Book # 2 - plac
due du

MW01615873

BROKEN

(A Casey Bolt FBI Suspense Thriller —Book 1)

Molly Black

Molly Black

Bestselling author Molly Black is author of the MAYA GRAY FBI suspense thriller series, comprising ten books (and counting); of the RYLIE WOLF FBI suspense thriller series, comprising six books; of the TAYLOR SAGE FBI suspense thriller series, comprising eight books; of the KATIE WINTER FBI suspense thriller series, comprising eleven books (and counting); of the RUBY HUNTER FBI suspense thriller series, comprising five books (and counting); of the CAITLIN DARE FBI suspense thriller series, comprising six books (and counting); of the REESE LINK mystery series, comprising six books (and counting); of the CLAIRE KING FBI suspense thriller series, comprising seven books (and counting); of the PIPER WOODS mystery series, comprising five books (and counting); of the GRACE FORD mystery series, comprising seven books (and counting); and of the CASEY BOLT mystery series, comprising five books (and counting).

An avid reader and lifelong fan of the mystery and thriller genres, Molly loves to hear from you, so please feel free to visit www.mollyblackauthor.com to learn more and stay in touch.

Copyright © 2023 by Molly Black. All rights reserved. Except as permitted under the U.S. Copyright Act of 1976, no part of this publication may be reproduced, distributed or transmitted in any form or by any means, or stored in a database or retrieval system, without the prior permission of the author. This ebook is licensed for your personal enjoyment only. This ebook may not be re-sold or given away to other people. If you would like to share this book with another person, please purchase an additional copy for each recipient. If you're reading this book and did not purchase it, or it was not purchased for your use only, then please return it and purchase your own copy. Thank you for respecting the hard work of this author. This is a work of fiction. Names, characters, businesses, organizations, places, events, and incidents either are the product of the author's imagination or are used fictionally. Any resemblance to actual persons, living or dead, is entirely coincidental.
ISBN: 978-1-0943-9634-7

BOOKS BY MOLLY BLACK

CASEY BOLT MYSTERY SERIES
BROKEN (Book #1)
FLAWED (Book #2)
BLEMISHED (Book #3)
DAMAGED (Book #4)
TWISTED (Book #5)

GRACE FORD MYSTERY SERIES
NEARLY MINE (Book #1)
NEARLY SAFE (Book #2)
NEARLY FREE (Book #3)
NEARLY GONE (Book #4)
NEARLY HIS (Book #5)

CLAIRE KING MYSTERY SERIES
ONCE HE SEES (Book #1)
ONCE HE LONGS (Book #2)
ONCE HE TAKES (Book #3)
ONCE HE FEELS (Book #4)
ONCE HE KNOWS (Book #5)

MAYA GRAY MYSTERY SERIES
GIRL ONE: MURDER (Book #1)
GIRL TWO: TAKEN (Book #2)
GIRL THREE: TRAPPED (Book #3)
GIRL FOUR: LURED (Book #4)
GIRL FIVE: BOUND (Book #5)
GIRL SIX: FORSAKEN (Book #6)
GIRL SEVEN: CRAVED (Book #7)
GIRL EIGHT: HUNTED (Book #8)
GIRL NINE: GONE (Book #9)

RYLIE WOLF FBI SUSPENSE THRILLER

FOUND YOU (Book #1)
CAUGHT YOU (Book #2)
SEE YOU (Book #3)
WANT YOU (Book #4)
TAKE YOU (Book #5)
DARE YOU (Book #6)

TAYLOR SAGE FBI SUSPENSE THRILLER
DON'T LOOK (Book #1)
DON'T BREATHE (Book #2)
DON'T RUN (Book #3)
DON'T FLINCH (Book #4)
DON'T REMEMBER (Book #5)
DON'T TELL (Book #6)

KATIE WINTER FBI SUSPENSE THRILLER
SAVE ME (Book #1)
REACH ME (Book #2)
HIDE ME (Book #3)
BELIEVE ME (Book #4)
HELP ME (Book #5)
FORGET ME (Book #6)
HOLD ME (Book #7)
PROTECT ME (Book #8)
REMEMBER ME (Book #9)
CATCH ME (Book #10)
WATCH ME (Book #11)

RUBY HUNTER FBI SUSPENSE THRILLER
IF I RUN (Book #1)
IF I TELL (Book #2)
IF I LIVE (Book #3)
IF I FORGET (Book #4)
IF I RETURN (Book #5)

CAITLIN DARE FBI SUSPENSE THRILLER
COME GET ME (Book #1)
COME FIND ME (Book #2)
COME TAKE ME (Book #3)
COME CATCH ME (Book #4)

COME SAVE ME (Book #5)

REESE LINK MYSTERY
BEYOND REASON (Book #1)
BEYOND REACH (Book #2)
BEYOND REPAIR (Book #3)
BEYOND DOUBT (Book #4)
BEYOND NORMAL (Book #5)

PROLOGUE

Even beauty held dark secrets.

And the sommelier's workspace was no exception.

The wine-tasting studio was a symphony of elegance and refinement, awash in the warm glow of soft lighting that danced off the gold-leaf accents adorning the walls. Rows upon rows of wine bottles nestled in their mahogany racks, their labels a kaleidoscope of colors, each telling a story from vineyards across the globe. The air in the room was heavy with the inviting aroma of aged oak and the subtle hints of the myriad flavors locked within the bottles.

It was into this sanctum that the sommelier stepped to open for the early morning, her confident strides betraying her expertise and passion for wine. As she crossed the threshold, she paused to take in the familiar scene, her eyes scanning the meticulously arranged rows with a discerning gaze. She was a woman who had dedicated herself to the pursuit of excellence in her craft, and every aspect of the studio bore testament to her unwavering commitment.

"Another day in paradise," she murmured to herself, allowing a small smile to tug at the corners of her lips as she adjusted her glasses. It was the small details that truly made the difference, she mused, as she reached out to straighten a bottle label that was ever so slightly askew. Each movement was deliberate and precise, carried out with the same care and attention that she lavished upon the wines she so expertly selected.

As she moved further into the studio, she could not help but feel a swell of pride bubble up within her. This was more than just a job for her; it was a calling, a passion that consumed her waking hours and haunted her dreams. Every wine she chose was a reflection of her own taste and judgment, a carefully curated selection that represented the best the world had to offer.

"Time to work your magic," she whispered, running her fingers lightly over the row of wine glasses, each one polished to perfection and waiting to be filled with the nectar.

She liked coming early--the only one in the studio.

It gave her a sense of... perspective.

The silence of the studio enveloped her like a shroud, wrapping itself around her as she walked further into the room. The only sound that punctuated the quiet was the rhythmic echo of her footsteps against the polished oak floors, each step resonating through the empty space. It was in moments like these, when the world seemed to hold its breath, that she felt most... unique.

But also, sometimes, out here in the desolate mountains north of Seattle...

Isolated. Vulnerable.

She hesitated, wondering if the distant creaking sound was just the wind.

"Hello?" she called out hesitantly, half-hoping for a response, though she knew it was unlikely. The studio was her sanctuary, a place where she could lose herself in the world of wine without interruption or distraction. And yet, there was a part of her that longed for company, for someone with whom she could share her passion and expertise.

As she continued to make her way through the studio, her eyes fell upon one of the doors leading to the storage area.

The door was open.

She stared. Blinked.

It didn't change the fact that the door was open.

Now she *knew* she'd locked that.

A small knot of unease began to form in her stomach as she noticed the lock was disengaged.

"Is anyone there?" she asked, trying to keep the tremor from her voice as she glanced nervously around the room. Her heart began to race, and she couldn't shake the feeling that unseen eyes were watching her every move. "This isn't funny," she muttered under her breath, forcing herself to take slow, measured breaths as she attempted to regain her composure.

She took a step towards the door, her hand reaching out to close it and engage the lock. But as her fingers brushed against the cool metal, she hesitated.

"Get a grip," she chided herself, shaking her head at her own irrational fears. "You're letting your imagination run wild." And with a deep, steadying breath, she tugged the door open, and stepped inside.

Another long, dark room, lined with vats.

The walls bare, but the room smelling sweet--the scent of grapes fermenting.

With each echoing step across the polished floors, the sommelier couldn't shake the prickling sensation that crawled up the back of her neck. Her fingers twitched at her side as she tried to focus on the task at hand, but her thoughts were scattered and uneasy. The unlocked door had unnerved her more than she cared to admit.

"Maybe I should call someone," she muttered, pausing mid-step. "No, no, don't be silly," she scolded herself almost immediately. "It's just a door." Yet, even as she attempted to brush off her worries, her heart continued to race within her chest, matching the tempo of her footsteps.

As she walked deeper into the studio, her eyes flickered from one end of the room to the other. She tried to immerse herself in the familiar sights and smells of the wine-tasting studio – the rows of gleaming bottles, the rich aroma of aged oak – but it wasn't enough to quiet her unease.

"Focus," she whispered under her breath, closing her eyes for a brief moment. "You've got work to do."

Her gaze snapped to the far corner of the long hall filled with vats; something unusual – a faint glow illuminating the farthest corner of the hall. Curiosity piqued, she squinted, trying to discern the source of the light. It seemed to be coming from the area where the largest vats were stored – an area that was typically shrouded in darkness.

"Is someone there?" she called out hesitantly, her voice barely above a whisper. The only response was the echo of her own words, bouncing off the walls and amplifying her growing anxiety.

"Okay, okay," she murmured, taking a deep breath to steady her nerves. "Just go check it out. It's probably nothing." With each hesitant step towards the faint glow, the sommelier couldn't help but feel as though she was walking on a tightrope, teetering between rationality and all-consuming fear.

Her thoughts raced, grappling with the growing tension in her chest. "It could be an electrical issue," she reasoned, trying to convince herself that there was a logical explanation for the unexplained light. "Or maybe someone left a flashlight on." Yet, even as she clung to these rationalizations, the gnawing sense of dread continued to grow, like a dark cloud looming above her.

"Should I call the police?" she muttered under her breath, her fingers fumbling with the phone in her pocket. "But what if it's nothing? I'll look like a fool." Her heart hammered against her ribcage, each beat screaming at her to take action, to do something to quell the mounting fear.

3

"Hello?" she called out again, louder this time, hoping to rouse any potential intruders. But once more, silence was her only answer. Swallowing hard, she steeled herself and pressed on, the faint light drawing her deeper into the bowels of the wine-tasting studio.

With one final deep breath, she rounded the side of the large vat, and her eyes fell on the source of the light.

A watch.

A beeping, glowing watch.

One of those smartwatches, and it was clearly malfunctioning.

But it wasn't the watch, per se, which had snared her attention.

There, draped over the side of one of the large vats, was a hand – a human hand – soaked in wine and dripping onto the floor below. Its fingers were limp, lifeless, and stained a dark crimson.

She stared in horror, her mouth unhinged and her ears hurt.

Why did her ears hurt?

It took a second to realize it was from the sound of her own scream.

CHAPTER ONE

Casey Bolt sat in the Lamaze class, wishing she hadn't been forced to wear the fake pregnancy belly.

It itched, for one.

And with her, even the slightest sense on her skin could have ramifications for her *other* senses.

She shifted uncomfortably, twisting at the velcro strap wrapped under her protruding shirt.

Around her, the other women in the class were following the instructor's calm, soothing directives.

"How's it going?" said the voice in her earpiece.

She bent over, touching her toes as best she could, pretending as if she were engaging in the stretches with the rest of the women in the small room.

But Casey brushed her dark hair out of her eyes, using this as an excuse to mutter, "Awful."

"One of them's the killer. We narrowed it down," said the voice of her partner in her ear. "Just gotta find which one."

"Why don't you come in here," she said, her tone testy.

"Not sure they'd like a man showing up in a pregnancy class," her partner, Nathan, chortled.

Casey just sighed, and turned to scan the room again.

It was hard to imagine any of these women as a cold-blooded murderer.

But there it was--the financial clue they'd found on the receipt in the last victim's wallet had led them here.

Someone in this class had killed two women.

But who?"

"Alright, class, now breathe slowly," said the instructor, her bronze skin sparkling and her bright, white smile glowing under the soft lighting.

Casey took a deep breath, trying to calm her racing thoughts. She couldn't afford to lose focus, not when they were so close to catching the killer.

As the instructor continued with the breathing exercises, Casey's eyes scanned the room once more, studying each woman's face for any sign of guilt or deceit.

Her gaze fell on a woman in the corner, her arms tightly crossed over her chest, her eyes darting around the room as if looking for an escape.

Then again, maybe she just had to pee.

"Okay, everyone, let's take a break," the instructor announced, clapping her hands together. "Grab some water and stretch your legs."

As the women began to chat and move about the room, Casey slowly made her way towards the woman in the corner.

As she approached, Casey winced, the velcro still scratching at her skin.

It was a gift and a curse.

She didn't *sense* things the way most people did. As a Synesthete, Casey had the unique experience of

being able to see sounds as colors, taste words, and feel emotions as physical sensations. It made her a great detective, but it also made her hypersensitive to external stimuli, like the scratchy velcro on her fake pregnancy belly.

"Hi there," Casey said, trying to sound friendly as she approached the woman. "Are you feeling okay?"

The woman's eyes darted up to meet Casey's, her expression guarded. "Yeah, I'm fine," she replied curtly.

Casey studied her for a moment, taking in the woman's tense posture and guarded demeanor. "I'm sorry to bother you, but I couldn't help but notice that you seem a bit on edge," she said, her voice gentle. "Is there anything you want to talk about?"

The woman hesitated for a moment, her eyes flickering around the room as if searching for an escape. "I don't know what you're talking about," she finally said, her voice barely above a whisper.

Casey sighed.

Her palm was now itching. Her right palm.

An incessant, almost scratching feeling.

Anxiety. Nerves.

She could pick up this woman's emotions, and it was playing out in Casey's own nerve endings.

She rubbed her hand absentmindedly against her cushioned belly.

Casey Bolt stood amidst the cluster of expectant mothers, their faces glowing with the promise of new life. The air was thick with anticipation as each woman practiced her breathing exercises, even during the break, as if somehow they didn't want to miss even the smallest window to care for their younglings, while also mingling and clinging to the reassurance that they were not alone in this journey. Casey felt a pang of guilt for her deception but pushed it aside, reminding herself that she was there to catch a killer. The Lamaze class had been infiltrated by an imposter, and it was her job to find out who it was.

"Alright, while we take our break, how about we try another round of deep breaths," the instructor encouraged, her soothing voice guiding the women through the techniques she'd taught them. "In through your nose, and out through your mouth." Casey followed suit, mimicking the synchronized inhalations and exhalations around her.

The woman leaned forward, studying Casey and whispering, "I have to go."

Casey stared at her. "What?"

And now, up close, she realized the anxiety, the discomfort... it was due to pain. She could see it in the way the woman grimaced.

"I think... I think I'm in labor!" the woman said.

The moment she spoke, another woman, standing nearby, named Candace, exclaimed, "April is in labor!"

A squawk of excitement arose from the gathered group. Two of the older women, self-appointed chaperones of the group, went on either side of April, and gently guided her out of the room.

"What's going on?" the voice in her earpiece insisted.

But she sighed, shaking her head.

"No go. I was wrong. She's in labor."

"Shit. Alright. Well--who else is there?"

Casey turned once more to examine the occupants of the small room. Only about ten remained. Each of them was once more focused on the instructor who was standing at the front of the room, flashing that million dollar smile, and nodding.

"Good job, ladies," the instructor praised, a genuine smile gracing her lips. "Remember, practice makes perfect. The more you work on your breathing techniques, the better prepared you'll be for labor."

Casey nodded, forcing a smile onto her face as she mentally catalogued each of the women in the room. They all appeared to be genuinely pregnant, their swollen bellies and tired expressions belying the immense strain they were under. Yet, one of them was hiding a dangerous secret, and it was up to Casey to uncover it before another life was lost.

"Blue Dress, six o'clock," Agent Nathan Hayes' voice echoed in Casey's earpiece, his words crisp and clear despite the faint static that accompanied them.

He was watching through the window, sitting in the SUV in the parking lot.

She glanced towards the window first, but couldn't see her partner behind the tinted glass.

He could clearly see her, however.

She glanced over her shoulder, eyes narrowing at the woman in question who was sipping from a water bottle by the window.

"Got her," Casey murmured, gaze flitting back to the instructor as she discreetly adjusted the white glove on her left hand.

She often wore gloves. It helped to calm her, so her skin wasn't always reacting to heat or texture or rigidity.

She also wore her dark hair back in a pony-tail--it sounded silly to most, but the way her hair would brush across her cheeks if she wore it forward was a huge distraction to her.

She didn't wear perfume, either. Only scentless soap.

"She's been taking pictures of everyone," Nathan said. "She keeps hiding the phone cam when someone looks over."

Casey's eyes narrowed as she peered at the woman in the blue dress.

Casey took a deep breath, her borrowed pregnancy bump pressing against her diaphragm. As an FBI agent, she had gone undercover countless times before, but this case felt different – more urgent, more dangerous. The killer they were hunting had already claimed two lives, and if Casey didn't succeed in unmasking them tonight, there would undoubtedly be more bloodshed.

"Alright, let's get back to it," the instructor called, clapping her hands together with a resounding smack. The women in the room obediently returned to their mats, eager to continue their Lamaze training in preparation for the births of their children.

As the instructor guided the pregnant women through another breathing exercise, Casey sensed her opportunity. The room buzzed with life, and she could feel the colors of their emotions ripple around her like an intricate tapestry. But she focused on Blue Dress – the woman had her camera out again, and was surreptitiously taking pictures once more.

"Okay, Cas," Nathan's voice whispered in her ear. "Should I come in?"

"Not yet," she murmured.

With practiced ease, she removed her glove, allowing her sensitive skin to be exposed. Casey feigned a stumble, brushing past the suspected woman. Her gloved fingers trailed lightly across the sleeve of Blue Dress's blouse, careful not to draw attention. As the fabric slid beneath her touch, an electric pulse of information surged into her mind.

"Wait," she thought, her eyes narrowing as her synesthesia worked its magic. She tasted the bitterness of disappointment and saw the color gray swirl around her.

The woman glanced at Casey, winced and stammered, "S-sorry. I... just was trying to remember how..." she trailed off, and looked embarrassed.

Not guilty. Embarrassed.

Casey spotted the picture.

It wasn't of the women in the room. No. It was of the diagrams and pictures on the wall. Each one showing step-by-step guides to what to expect on delivery day.

"I'm just nervous," Blue Dress said, wincing.

Casey flashed a quick smile of her own.

"Sorry," she murmured, already slipping her glove back on her hand.

Back at the department, she had caught flack from previous partners who hadn't seen her mental wiring as anything other than a burden.

But Nathan Hayes was different--the two of them had worked together for nearly three years now.

And they'd developed one of the best case closer rates in the Seattle field office.

As Casey's gaze swept across the room, her synesthesia-tinged senses flickered, each detail melding into the next. Her eyes settled on the instructor, a woman in her mid-thirties with short-cropped red hair and an air of authority that commanded attention. A sudden shift in the hues before her stirred something within Casey, a series of connections forming in her mind like a complex puzzle taking shape.

"Wait a minute," she murmured to Nathan through the comms, her voice barely more than a whisper. "I think I've got something."

"Go on, Cas," he urged, his own anticipation palpable even through the electronic connection.

"Think about it," she said, piecing together the fragments of information she'd gathered while observing the class. She whispered, but her voice was urgent, "The instructor has access to everyone's personal files. She could easily determine who was most vulnerable."

9

"The instructor?"

"Yeah," Casey said. "The receipt... the payment to the class. Maybe it was on the instructor because she'd kept hold of it after receiving payment from a client."

"Okay," Nathan conceded, "but do you have anything solid, anything we can use?"

"Her clothes," Casey breathed, excitement bubbling in her chest. "It's the same fabric we found at the crime scenes. It's a type of burlap with a cross-weave pattern. She's our killer."

"You sure?"

"Pretty darn."

But then, the instructor said something, and the women began to rise to their feet. "Class is over, Nate," she whispered urgently, her eyes never leaving the instructor. "The women are starting to leave. We need to move now."

"Copy that. I'm on my way," he replied.

As her pulse raced, each beat sending vibrant colors dancing before her eyes, Casey knew she couldn't afford to lose sight of the true killer.

The moment the Lamaze class ended, the instructor briskly walked towards the back exit, her eyes darting around with a newfound anxiety.

Casey followed out into the hall, where she nearly bumped into Nathan Hayes.

Nathan had a rugged and charismatic appearance, from his scruff to his salt-and-pepper dash of fringe. He had dark blue eyes that were nearly gray, and his hands had tattoos on the knuckles, spelling out the word *Bless*.

"Stay close, Cas," Nathan whispered as the two of them fell into step side-by-side.

Both of them moving after the instructor who had reached the end of the hall.

Casey's heart pounded in her chest as she followed the fleeing instructor, her legs propelling her forward. The weight of the fake belly-padding shifted around uncomfortably, making it difficult for her to maintain her speed.

The chase wove through the dimly lit hallways of the community center. Casey's gloves brushed against the cool metal railing, sending vivid green sparks dancing before her eyes.

"Where are we?" Nathan whispered. "I don't remember this from the blueprints."

"East hallway, approaching the gym," Casey panted, her breaths shallow but focused.

The instructor finally paused, glancing back at them.

She froze, staring.

Casey and Ethan also went still.

For a moment, silent communication passed between them.

The woman standing there hesitated, swallowing. Her fingers tensed--those same fingers that had snuffed the life out of two women and their unborn children.

Then, the woman with the bright white smile cursed and broke into a dead sprint.

"Nothing says guilty," Nathan started.

"Like running!" Casey finished, already breaking into a sprint after their fleeing suspect.

She burst after the suspect, shouting, "Rear exit. Cut her off at the rear exit!"

The instructor whirled around, wide-eyed, panic in her eyes. She tried to juke left, but Casey didn't stop. She guessed the feint and slammed headfirst into the suspect, tackling her to the ground.

CHAPTER TWO

Casey Bolt entered the FBI office, her wet hair clinging to her face like dark tendrils. Despite the rain-soaked morning and the weight of her damp ponytail, a genuine smile graced her lips. She stepped into the familiar hum of activity, pausing for a moment to take it all in.

Smiles were turned in her direction. She even received a thumbs up from Jerry-the tech guy.

"Good job, Bolt," he said.

She grinned back.

"Perp here?"

"At the local station," she replied. 'Confessed the moment we cuffed her."

Jerry the tech guy grinned even wider. A woman, Adelaide, Casey thought her name was, nodded in appreciation as she faxed something near a large, white machine.

Casey tried not to bask in the positive attention from her coworkers. But it was difficult.

Another successful case.

She walked through the maze of desks, Casey recalled the intricate web of connections she'd woven to crack the case.

It had taken *years* for the FBI to see her gifting as something other than a handicap.

But now...

Each piece of evidence had been a splash of color, a vivid hue that only she could perceive. Her synesthesia had been both a gift and a curse—constantly bombarded by sensory information, she'd learned to cocoon herself in long sleeves and gloves, to control the chaos within. But in moments like this, she reveled in the beauty of her own mind.

Even as the thought ocurred to her, she felt a flush of embarssment. She didn't want to think of herself as haughty--but she also knew what it was to be mentally... untypical.

A ripple of hushed conversation followed her, but she didn't mind. They were beginning to understand her, to appreciate the value of her unique perspective. It was more than she could have hoped for when she first joined the bureau.

The door to her small, cluttered office loomed ahead, and Casey hesitated before opening it. With her gloves on, she couldn't feel the cool metal of the doorknob, but she knew it was there. She took a deep breath, inhaling the scentless air that she'd grown accustomed to, and turned the handle.

Inside, her desk was a testament to her recent success—case files stacked high, photographs of key evidence pinned to the walls. Casey's eyes lingered on each piece as she mentally traced the colorful threads that had linked them all together into one complete tapestry.

She sank into her worn office chair and allowed herself a moment to bask in the satisfaction of her accomplishment.

She sent a quick text to Nathan, who'd agreed to stay back and help process the suspect. It was his turn, and after the case with the biker who smelled of BO, she was perfectly content to let him have at it.

Still, the text she sent read: *Way to go! You killed it out there!*

She hesitated, wrinkled her nose and added *metaphorically.*

She sent the message, felt awkward all of a sudden, but pushed aside the intrusive thought. The hum of the FBI office buzzed through the open door of her office, a cacophony of ringing phones and clacking keyboards that melded into a symphony of productivity.

As Casey sat at her desk, she flipped through a stack of case files, absentmindedly.

But no sooner than she'd released a long, pent up breath, then her phone vibrated in her pocket. She glanced down at the screen, catching a glimpse of an unknown number before hastily shoving the device back into her pocket.

"Casey!" called out a stern voice from across the room, cutting through her thoughts like a blade. It belonged to Director Johnson, a man who had made no secret of his disdain for Casey's unorthodox methods.

She looked through her open door to see Johnson standing there, tapping his watch. He gestured impatiently for her to approach his office, his eyebrows furrowed in disapproval.

Her gloved fingers curled into fists by her sides, the leather's familiar texture providing a small measure of comfort. Despite the nods of approval she had received earlier, it was clear that not everyone shared in the celebration of her recent success.

She walked hastily across the room towards Johnson's office.

He was once again sitting behind his desk as she arrived.

"Take a seat, Bolt," Director Johnson ordered gruffly, without looking up from his desk. The tension in the room was palpable, a storm cloud hovering just overhead. As Casey eased into the chair opposite him, she tried to suppress her unease by focusing on the colors that swirled around Johnson in her synesthetic perception—dark blues and grays, a reflection of his mood.

"Sir?" she asked tentatively, her voice low and steady despite her racing pulse. The director finally met her gaze, his eyes cold and unyielding.

"Your track record speaks for itself, Bolt," he admitted begrudgingly, "but don't let it go to your head. You're here to do a job, just like everyone else." The implication was clear: she may have won the battle, but the war for acceptance was far from over.

"Understood, sir," Casey replied, her voice betraying no hint of emotion. Inside, though, her thoughts churned like a turbulent sea, caught between pride and frustration. "I... I don't understand. Is there a new case?"

He just grunted.

With a practiced hand, he flipped open a file on his desk.

"Early this morning, a body was discovered drowned in a vat of wine at a local winery," he said, his eyes never leaving the grisly photographs in front of him. "The victim is Jamie Stevens, a well-known wine connoisseur. The scene is...unusual, to say the least."

"Who would drown someone in wine?" Casey murmured, her voice tinged with a mixture of disbelief and curiosity. Her fingers tapped rhythmically on the armrests as she visualized the scene, her synesthesia transforming the gruesome details into an intricate tapestry of colors and sensations.

"Your guess is as good as mine," Johnson replied, finally looking up from the file. His gaze was piercing, as though daring Casey to unravel the mystery in front of them. "But while I disapprove of your methods, I can't disapprove of your record: I have at least some confidence in your ability to find the answers, Bolt. Especially Hayes."

Nathan had always been favored by Johnson. Casey wasn't sure why, and she'd decided long ago that speculation would only hurt the matter.

For a moment, Casey felt the weight of his words settle on her shoulders like a heavy cloak.

She had no doubt that he *intended* her to feel the pressure.

Johnson was the only boss who'd given her poor marks on her last three performance reviews.

The pressure was there, but she had never been one to shy away from a challenge. She clenched her jaw.

"Thank you, sir," she said, her voice firm and resolute. "We won't let you down."

"See that you don't," Johnson warned.

As Casey left Johnson's office, she found Nathan waiting for her, his tall frame leaning against the wall with an air of casual confidence. He looked up from his phone, his chiseled features breaking into a grin upon seeing her. "Ready to dive into another case?" he asked, his tone light yet earnest.

"More than ready," Casey replied, her eyes shimmering with determination as she shared an affirming nod with her partner.

He smirked.

"What?"

"Johnson got you pissed again?"

She frowned.

He just shrugged and gave her a firm pat on the back. It would've hurt if she hadn't already braced herself for it, having expected it.

Hayes was predictable in such things.

For one, he was also wearing his street clothes. A hoody, jeans. That was it. His hair was slicked back, and his casually good looks did little to lift the air of a lazy tom cat.

He was smirking at her even as he fiddled with a cigarette in one hand.

He didn't smoke it, as he'd quit years ago.

But he liked how it felt.

She, more than anyone, understood the comfort of tactile pleasure.

"Oh, you know," she said, shrugging, "the usual. Doesn't trust my abilities, but trusts my track record."

"Same ol' schtick?" Hayes twirled the cigarette between his fingers like a band leader.

She nodded as the two of them moved out the front door again.

"She confess at the station too?"

"In writing."

"Damn. Did she say why she did it?"

"Jealousy," Hayes replied, tossing a piece of gum into his mouth. The scent of mint lingered on the air.

Casey could *hear* faint choir bells. Sometimes scents aroused auditory cues.

She'd once solved a case involving a master burglar based on cologne alone.

15

The two of them took the stairs hurriedly, moving towards the bottom floor.

"You read the file on your phone?"

"Skimmed it," Hayes said.

"You know, they give us that stuff to read."

"That's what I got you for. Your young eyes are better for that whole reading business."

She rolled her eyes. "I'm thirty, Nathan."

"Yeh, a whippersnapper."

"You're incorigable."

"Incori-what?" He shook his head. "Don't know Greek, Bolt. I'm driving."

Before she could protest, the incorrigible agent slipped into the front seat of their waiting SUV.

She didn't make a fuss of it.

He was brash, and a bit rough around the edges, but nice enough to look at, and fiercely loyal.

He'd had her back on more than one occasion.

She felt, though she wouldn't say it *too* loudly, that if not for him, her career with the FBI might not have made it past the first sniff test.

So she settled in the passenger seat, pulling out her own phone to studiously commit the case file to memory.

Jamie Stevens, drowned in a vat of wine.

She paused. "Oh, wow."

"What?" he said.

"The vineyard and tasting studio. It's *Amma's Secret*."

"So?"

"It's like... a really exclusive place."

"They got Bic-macs?"

"No."

"Not interested."

"Well, we're heading there anyway."

Nathan shrugged, and he scanned the roadside, likely looking for a place to buy big-macs.

Casey just returned her attention to her screen, reading intently and feeling a cold shiver move down her spine as they cut through the heart of Seattle, heading towards the mountains in the distance.

CHAPTER THREE

With every fiber of his being screaming for him to turn and flee, the man remained rooted to the spot, unable to tear his eyes away from the sight of the cop cars and the officers who moved like ghosts through the vineyard.

Shadows crept like tendrils, wrapping around the edges of the vineyard as dusk settled in. The air was heavy with anticipation, and the faint scent of ripe grapes lingered, blending with the earthy dampness of the soil. In the distance, the silhouette of a man stood beneath the twisted branches of an ancient oak tree, his gaze fixed on the scene unfolding before him.

The man's breath caught in his throat as he watched the cop cars parked at the edge of the vineyard. Their vibrant red and blue lights pierced the darkness, casting a tapestry of images against the rows of grapevines. From his hidden vantage point, he could feel the tension in the air, thick and palpable like a storm cloud ready to burst.

His heart hammered against his chest, the adrenaline coursing through his veins as he observed the officers moving about, their flashlights casting long shadows across the ground. He couldn't hear their words, but he didn't need to; he knew all too well the gravity of the situation unfolding before him.

As he continued to watch, the man found himself transfixed by the contrast between the darkness that enveloped him and the vibrant scene playing out at the vineyard. Shadows seemed to dance along the rows of vines, as if they too were captivated by the spectacle. It was a juxtaposition that both intrigued and unnerved him, and he couldn't help but wonder what role he played in this strange tableau.

Though he stood removed from the chaos, the man felt the weight of each passing second pressing down upon him, threatening to suffocate him in its crushing embrace.

He knew that he should leave. He should *definitely* leave.

He felt an odd mixture of fear and fascination as he watched the officers move through the vineyard, their flashlights casting long tendrils of light that snaked through the vines. A cold sweat broke out on his brow, and he wiped it away with a trembling hand, attempting to stifle the sob that threatened to escape his lips.

Though he tried to hold back the tide of tears, they came unbidden, streaming down his cheeks in rivulets. His heart ached with a strange longing that he could not quite name, and he found himself weeping silently in the shadows, a lone figure caught between the darkness and the light.

The man reached into the darkness beside him, his fingers brushing against the cold metal of an ornate cup. It was a relic from another time, a vestige of lost grandeur that seemed to hold secrets of its own. With trembling hands, he brought it to his lips, taking a slow, deliberate sip, as if imbibing the very mysteries that surrounded him.

The cup's contents, rich and intoxicating in their complexity, washed over his tongue like a wave of sensations. The flavors of ripe grapes and damp earth mingled with subtler hints of spice and oak, each element weaving together to form a tapestry of taste that mirrored the intricate patterns engraved upon the cup itself.

He'd paid a steep price for this cup.

For what was in it.

So had another--a soul.

He felt a slow shiver at the thought, and more tears came unbidden to his eyes.

"Shit," he whispered. "Dammit."

His ears strained to pick up every sound, from the distant wail of sirens echoing through the night to the rustle of leaves dancing in the breeze. The scent of the vineyard enveloped him, a heady mix of ripe fruit and dark, fertile soil that seemed to seep into his very soul.

"Hey! Hey, excuse me, sir!"

A voice called out from the path leading towards him. He spun towards it, eyes wide.

A figure was approaching, waving a hand silently.

A cop?

Hard to say.

He had to *leave.* Now.

He'd be back.

But not yet.

Not now. "Excuse me, sir--"

The man grabbed his cup, turned and bolted, sprinting off into the dark without a second glance back.

CHAPTER FOUR

The tires of Casey's sleek black car crunched over the gravel driveway as she and Nathan arrived at the crime scene in northern Washington.

They exchanged a tense glance before stepping out into the cool air, their breaths visible.

As they approached the vineyard, Casey couldn't help but marvel at the lush surroundings. The vibrant colors of the grapevines seemed to pop against the gray sky overhead, creating an intricate tapestry of deep purples, bright greens, and rich browns. She breathed in deeply, allowing the earthy scent of the soil to fill her nostrils, grounding her amidst the chaos of the investigation.

"Beautiful place," Nathan murmured, his eyes scanning the rows of vines as they walked.

"Hard to believe something so terrible happened here," Casey agreed, her gloved hands clenched tightly at her sides. Her synesthesia was already causing the mingling scents and colors to swirl together in her mind, playing like a symphony that only she could hear.

Ahead, they spotted police cars lining the road. There was a flash of lights.

Behind her, somewhere, Casey heard a voice calling out in the forest. "Excuse me, sir! Sir--wait!"

She glanced back, but didn't see anything.

She frowned, turning to approach the building where a man was standing between two cops, wringing his hands nervously.

The man looked something like a banker with a charcoal gray suit and a white shirt. He was thin and pale, with sharp features and slicked-back hair. Casey could see the beads of sweat on his forehead, and he spoke quickly.

"When are you going to clear out?" he was saying. "I've already lost an entire day of business. We can't make it two!"

Immediately, Casey pegged him as the owner or manager of the establishment.

19

She walked up to where the nervous little man was speaking to the police officers.

As she drew near, her foot scuffed against some concrete, and the man jolted, turning sharply to look at her.

"Excuse me, sir," Casey said in a calm voice, holding up her badge. "We're with the FBI. Can you tell me what happened here?"

It was a question she already knew the answer too, but one that was easy enough it could direct the man's focus to something beyond his own anxiety. Sometimes, that's all that was needed.

She could *taste* the anxiety. It had caused a faint charcoal tint on her tongue, and her heart went out to the nervous, frazzled man.

The man visibly relaxed when he saw the badge, but his anxiety was still evident in his voice as he spoke. "One of my employees found a body this morning. She called the police right away."

Casey nodded. "Thank you, sir. We appreciate your patience. Can you tell me anything about the victim? Do you have any idea who might have done this?"

The man shook his head quickly. "I don't know anything, I swear. We've had some issues with vandalism in the past, but nothing like this. I can't imagine who would do something so...horrible."

Casey could sense the man's fear and unease, and she knew that she would have to tread carefully if she wanted to get any useful information out of him.

The charcoal taste still lingered on her tongue.

"Where is the vat?" she said softly.

He waved a hand towards the open doors. "First hall--past the caution tape. Say," he added, "When do you think we will be able to open up again?"

Casey just smiled softly, patting him on the shoulder with one gloved hand.

"We'll try to speed this up, sir," she said.

And then she began to move, heading into the main building.

She spotted the hall with the caution tape, glanced at Nathan and the two of them ducked under it.

This section of the vineyard was empty.

The police were mainly gathered in the atrium as if scared of venturing back near where the body had been found.

It would've long since been removed, but the atmosphere was grim, and Casey could taste her own anxiety on the still air.

Ahead of them, Casey spotted wooden vats lined against the wall. The large barrels were stained with years of use, and Casey could see the dark red stains of wine on the ground around them.

As Casey and Nathan approached the large vat in the back corner, with caution tape encircling it, dangling between orange traffic cones, the air seemed to thicken with an ominous weight. Though the victim's body had been removed from the scene, the remnants of the gruesome act lingered like a ghostly presence. A stain on the ground spoke of where the body had been removed, allowing the wine-soaked corpse to leak onto the floor.

"Can you feel it?" Casey asked softly, her eyes scanning the area for any clues that might have been overlooked. Nathan nodded, his face grim as he surveyed the haunting scene before them.

Together, they began to comb through the area, their movements slow and deliberate as they searched for any signs of the killer's presence. Casey felt the familiar prickle of unease at the back of her neck, as though the very air around them was tinged with the remnants of fear and pain. She couldn't shake the feeling that they were being watched, their every move observed by unseen eyes.

She wasn't studying the vat--it would already have been examined. Rather, her eyes combed the dark recesses throughout the room.

"Anything?" Nathan called out to her when he spotted her pause by a window.

She was frowning at the wooden ledge.

Scrape marks on the glass... On the outside.

She leaned forward, touching the latch.

Broken.

"I may have found our killer's entry point," she murmured.

He approached, glancing at the ledge.

"Prints?"

She was already peering through the window.

"No--gravel."

"Shit."

She nodded in agreement. She pulled out her phone and took a picture of the latch, however.

She then paused, closing her eyes and inhaling slowly, allowing her synesthetic perceptions to guide her.

It was a unique gift, and not one that always yielded results. But if there was one thing she'd learned, it was to use *every* tool.

She inhaled slowly, exhaled, then breathed in again.

The scent in the air was a veritable tapestry of hues, coming from the open window and the closed hall; the earthy aroma of the soil outside painted broad strokes of deep, rich browns across her mental canvas. The vibrant green of the grapevines added another layer, intertwining with the other colors, merging and separating in a mesmerizing dance.

"Wait." Casey halted abruptly, her attention drawn to a subtle shift in the colorful symphony surrounding them. Swirling amidst the natural scentscape was a foreign note, a sinister streak of dark red that seemed out of place.

She frowned, looking around.

A perfume? A cologne?

It was a lingering, faint scent.

She shook her head, unsure what she was detecting.

She sighed, though, shaking her head. "I don't think I've smelled that before."

"Sorry," Nathan quipped.

"Funny," she replied. "You know, you make that joke a lot."

"If it ain't broke, don't fix it," Nathan said with a wink.

She rolled her eyes.

But the two of them were suddenly distracted as a figure waved at them from the door.

They both glanced over.

A cop was standing there, clearing his throat.

"Umm... the woman who found the body is waiting for you. Should I send her home?"

"No," Casey said quickly. "We're coming."

She shared a look with Nathan, and then the two of them approached the door, heading to speak with their first witness.

CHAPTER FIVE

As Casey and Nathan sat down at the live-edge table in the tasting studio, a young woman with eyes red and swollen from endless tears fidgeted uncomfortably on a seat in front of them. Her body trembled like a leaf caught in a gust of wind, and her hands clutched at a crumpled tissue as if it were her last lifeline.

"Ms. Alvarez?" Casey asked gently, leaning closer to the distraught woman. "We understand this is difficult, but we need your help."

The woman nodded, her breath hitching as she swallowed back fresh sobs. Casey's heart ached for her, but she was acutely aware that every moment counted.

Another difficulty of her gift was how she *felt* the emotions of others so strongly.

Compassion wasn't the most useful of tools when doggedly pursuing a killer.

It sometimes served a purpose, but often she thought it just got in the way.

And yet... She never wanted to turn it off. To see the people she spoke with *as people.* What was the point of investigating murders if she lost the value for those who were hurt by the predators she sought.

She focused on the task at hand, knowing that finding justice for the victim was the best way to ease this woman's pain.

"Can you tell us what you saw?" Nathan prompted, his voice soft but firm.

"I... I found her," Ms. Alvarez whispered, her voice barely audible. "In the vat... I can't get the image out of my head."

Casey observed the witness closely, noting the way she wrung her hands and shifted her weight in the chair, her fingers peeling at the live edge of the wooden table, but finding only lacquer. Fear radiated off her in palpable waves, mingling with an earthy green scent that reminded Casey of freshly cut grass.

Casey didn't always know what the senses were; she had a memory catalogue of past experiences, but sometimes her brain wired things in unique ways. She'd learned to not chase every unique thought.

"Did you notice anything unusual before you found the body?" Casey asked.

Ms. Alvarez hesitated for a moment, her gaze darting around the vineyard. "I did see someone leaving... in a hurry," she finally admitted, the words tumbling out in a rush.

"Who was it?"

"The manager," she said quickly. "Gabe Vincente."

She spoke the name quickly, and there was a note of severity in her voice.

Casey leaned back, crossing her arms. "Did you get along with Mr. Vincente?"

Ms. Alvarez glanced towards the door, hesitated, and then swallowed. "He's my boss," she said.

"That doesn't exactly answer my question."

"Yeah, well... I need this job," she muttered.

Casey and Nathan exchanged a knowing look. They had encountered this type of witness before - someone who was too scared to speak the truth because they feared retaliation.

"Ms. Alvarez, we understand your fear, but we need to know the truth. Was there anything about Mr. Vincente's behavior or actions that struck you as strange or suspicious?" Nathan asked, his tone gentle but persistent.

Ms. Alvarez fidgeted with her tissue, her eyes darting around the room as if searching for an escape. "He's been acting weird lately," she finally admitted, her voice barely above a whisper.

"Weird how?" Casey asked, leaning forward.

"He's been... I don't know, more aggressive than usual. Yelling at us for no reason, making unreasonable demands. And... and he's been drinking a lot more," she said, her voice cracking with emotion.

Casey and Nathan exchanged another look. The pieces were starting to fall into place - a manager with anger issues and a drinking problem, a witness who was too scared to speak up, and a victim found in a vat.

"He also... he was strange around us."

"Us?" Casey asked. "The employees?" Suddenly, Casey felt her face warming up. She hesitated, then realized what her subconscious was picking up on.

Embarrassment.

"No, around us women," said Ms. Alvarez quickly. "he would make passes at most of us. I felt it was harmless enough..." She shrugged. "But he could be persistent."

"And the victim; did you know Jamie Stevens?"

A quick shake of the head. "Never seen her before in my life."

"You're sure?" Casey pulled out a DMV photo that had been provided.

She turned the image towards Alvarez.

Alvarez leaned in and shuddered. "She was very pretty," the woman said softly.

Casey glanced at the image as well. Pretty wasn't the word that came to mind. Jamie Stevens was a pleasant-looking woman. But her features were more *kind* than attractive in any physical sort of way.

She had short blonde hair, cut in a bob, and a smile that seemed to light up her entire face. Casey couldn't help but feel a pang of sadness for the victim. She didn't deserve to end up discarded like trash.

Nathan cleared his throat, breaking Casey out of her thoughts. "Ms. Alvarez, we appreciate your honesty. Is there anything else you can tell us that might help with the investigation?"

Ms. Alvarez shook her head. "No, I'm sorry. That's all I know."

Casey and Nathan thanked her and stood up to leave. As they walked out of the interview room, Casey couldn't help but feel a sense of frustration.

It took her a second to realize she was picking up on Nathan's tense posture and flower.

"What?" she said.

Her partner just frowned.

"I don't like guys that go after their employees."

She studied him, hesitant. "Seems oddly specific."

He just waved a hand. "Nah, it's not... not just that. Anyone who has power. You know. Uses it to be a creep."

She studied her partner. He was nearly a decade older, in his forties, but his eyes were now narrowed as if he were focused on something in the distance.

She remembered now, briefly, about reading how his mother had a rough life.

She hadn't seen much beyond bullet points, which had been provided in a file when the two of them had first partnered.

But she could tell this was personal for Nathan.

"Are you going to be able to speak with Mr. Vincente?"

"Huh? What? Yeah. Of course."

She studied him, and sighed, shrugging. She made a mental note to be careful when they spoke to the manager.

Hot tempers escalated things rather quickly.

As they reached the exit, she spotted the skinny, fidgety man who they'd spotted earlier.

He was now leaning against a walnut wooden post, smoking a cigarette with shaking hands.

"Definitely nervous," she said.

"Vincente!" called out Nathan.

The man looked up, confirming his identity.

The two of them approached the manager, and he took a long puff of his cigarette as he watched them draw nearer.

"Hello, sir," said Casey as she drew close. "Gabriel Vincente, yes?"

He hesitated, as if unsure how to respond to the use of his name. But then his head bobbed a single time.

"H-how can I help you?"

She studied him. "I'm not sure, sir. Maybe it's I who can help you."

"About what?"

"You'd mentioned you didn't know or see anything involving the body found on your property."

"I didn't!" he stared at her. "Is someone saying otherwise? Because if they are, they're a damn liar!"

His hands bunched at his sides.

She watched him, watching the way the light from inside the building danced across his features. His nose was sharp, and his eyes narrowed, giving him a look like a hawk.

His shoulders were hunched, though, and it reminded her more of a vulture.

She felt a strange itch on her right hand.

More anxiety.

She said, "You were seen leaving the premises in the morning."

"Shit. Is that what she's saying? Alvarez is a liar!"

She kept her tone pleasant, speculative. She didn't rise to the accusation.

Instead, she said, "And are you denying it?"

He paused, licking the corner of his lip and taking another puff of the cigarette.

Nathan was standing in front of the man now. And Hayes said, "Why don't you look at us when we talk to you, bud?"

He reached out and flicked the cigarette from the man's lips.

The manager was so shocked, he stood frozen for a minute, his fingers still raised in a Y where they'd been bracing the cigarette.

Casey watched as Gabriel Vincente's face flushed red with anger. "Who the hell do you think you are?" he spat out, his voice rising.

26

Nathan didn't back down. "Oh, you don't like it when people cross personal boundaries?" he raised an eyebrow.

If his insinuation was clear, Vincente didn't show it.

Instead he spluttered, shaking his head side to side.

"We hear you like coming on to your female employees," Hayes said quietly.

"Bullshit!"

Casey stepped between them, trying to diffuse the tension. "Let's all take a deep breath," she said. "Mr. Vincente, we're just trying to get to the bottom of what happened here. If you can help us, we can make sure this is all resolved quickly."

Casey held her breath as the manager's eyes flicked between her and Nathan, his expression twisting with anger. He spat out, "You think you can just come in here and treat me like some kind of criminal?"

Nathan didn't back down, his own gaze steady as he met the man's angry stare.

He snorted again, his arms crossed over his chest defensively. "Well, I don't know anything about any murder. And if you don't have any evidence, then I suggest you leave me alone."

"Getting defensive all of a sudden, aren't you?" Nathan said.

"No shit, Sherlock, and how would you act if someone came accusing you of all sortsa shit."

"You still haven't denied being here this morning."

"Yes, I did! And I will again. I wasn't."

"So you're saying if we have you on a camera, then it'd be mistaken?"

Casey was playing to her strengths. She knew he was feeling anxious--it was practically bleeding off of him. She could smell his fear.

And she glanced surreptitiously towards one of the cameras over the door.

Of course, she didn't have access to that footage.

Not yet.

Vincente, though, didn't need to know that.

He followed her gaze, stared, and then seemed to wilt.

His face went pale. "I... I was here. Maybe. Yeah. yeah, I forgot. just, you know. A long day."

"Forgot, huh?" Hayes said, his voice gruff. "Asshole," he added.

Casey winced. She'd grown accustomed to Nathan's rough-around-the-edges personality, but sometimes she felt he pushed it too far.

She glanced down towards where the discarded cigarette lay smoldering on the ground. Then, I looked back up at the manager.

"And what were you doing here this morning?"

"Checking the books. That's all."

"And you didn't hear anything?"

"Nothing!"

"How's that possible?"

"It's a big place. I was in my office. Back of the building. I... I can show you!" he said suddenly.

There was an edge to his voice. The emotions she felt coming off him didn't quite register with his attempt at a calming tone.

Casey exchanged a glance with Nathan before nodding. "Sure, that'd be helpful. Lead the way."

Vincente nodded, his face still pale, and began walking around the building. Casey and Nathan followed him, both keeping a watchful eye on their surroundings.

Ahead, she spotted a sports car parked over two handicapped spots.

"Like it?" Vincente said, noticing Nathan's appreciative gaze. "It's a new model. Just came out."

Nathan snorted. "Wine business pays well, I take it?"

"I do alright."

He was gesturing towards an Exit door in the back now. "This is where I came out. See," he added, turning to look at them. "On the sheer opposite side of the place. Besides, who knows when that lady was drowned."

Casey glanced at Nathan before speaking. "What makes you say that?"

Vincente's eyebrows rose as he shrugged. "Just a guess. I mean... I clearly didn't do it. And if she was drowned, it could've been after we closed at ten."

Nathan said, "Did you know the dead woman?"

"No clue."

"You sure about that?"

"Positive."

"You didn't ask me her name," said Nathan.

A pause, a flicker in the man's eyes.

"I... I was told earlier."

"What was it?"

"I don't remember."

"So how do you know you don't know her?" Nathan pressed.

The manager was flustered now.

"I'm telling you, I don't know her!"

Casey stepped forward. "Mr. Vincente, we're just trying to understand what happened here. If you don't know the victim, that's fine. We're just trying to get to the bottom of this. Can you help us do that?"

She was trying to calm the situation again, but this time, it didn't work.

He was only growing more agitated.

Nathan had the DMV photo of their victim up. He turned Ms. Stevens' picture towards the manager. "You didn't know her? You're sure."

For a moment, Vincente stared at the picture. He swallowed, and there was a flicker of... *guilt*? In his gaze.

He said, "I... I just..."

He stared at the image, and it was as if the picture stared back at him. He let out a small, huffing little breath.

And then, without warning, he turned on his heel and sprinted towards the car door.

Nathan lurched, but missed.

The sports' car lights flashed.

And Vincente flung himself into the open door.

Nathan was scrambling forward, but Casey grabbed his arm, yanking him back to avoid being turned to paste by the suddenly revving vehicle.

The bright red paint flashed, and the tires left marks on the ground as it swerved past them.

Vincente screamed something that Casey couldn't make out as he sped away from the federal agents.

CHAPTER SIX

Double-timing back to their own car seemed a blur of motion, even as the red sports car scythed up the switchback, tires squealing as it sped away.

Casey flung herself into the front seat of their own vehicle.

Her heart pounded in her chest, her breaths shallow and quick as she gripped the steering wheel of the unmarked police car. Her senses were on high alert; she could feel the texture of the worn leather beneath her gloves, the faint hum of the engine reverberating through her body, and the sharp tang of adrenaline in the air.

The hum of the engine vibrated through Casey's fingertips as she gripped the steering wheel, her eyes locked on the road ahead. Her synesthesia painted the world around her in vivid hues, the colors blending and shifting with each new sound from the chase. The screech of tires was a fierce, jagged red, while the roar of engines was a deep, rumbling blue.

"Left!" Nathan shouted beside her.

Casey swerved, narrowly avoiding a collision with an oncoming truck. The winding roads demanded every ounce of her focus; one wrong move, and they'd be off course or worse.

"Right up ahead!" Nathan called out again.

She took the turn, barely noticing the way the colors around her danced in response to their high-speed pursuit. Her pulse raced in tandem with the car's speedometer, her breaths coming in short, urgent bursts.

The red sports car was a blur ahead of them, but it moved cautiously at the turns, as if Vincente was uncertain of his own movements.

As Casey navigated the serpentine vineyard roads, silence pervaded the car as they barreled down the road, save for the occasional sound of tires squealing on pavement.

Nathan had partnered with her long enough to know that sounds were often a distraction to her mind.

Casey's breath hitched as she zeroed in on Gabriel Vincente's vehicle just ahead.

"Get ready," she warned Nathan, her eyes locked onto the target. Gabriel's car veered left, and Casey anticipated the move before it even happened. The colors swirled in her vision, a symphony of sound and sight that allowed her to stay one step ahead. She pushed the accelerator, closing the gap between them.

"Casey, be careful," Nathan cautioned, gripping the door handle as the distance closed rapidly.

In one swift motion, she calculated the precise moment to strike. As Gabriel's car swerved right, Casey steered into him, the impact knocking his vehicle off balance. Tires screeched and metal groaned as the two cars collided, the smell of burning rubber mixing with the sweet scent of the vineyards.

Gabriel's car careened off the road, spinning out of control before coming to a jarring halt amidst the lush green of the vineyard. Casey and Nathan's car skidded to a stop nearby, dust and gravel spitting from beneath the tires.

The smell of burning rubber assaulted her nostrils as she flung open the door, emerging amidst clouds of dust and gravel that seemed to hang in the air like an oppressive fog.

She approached Gabriel's motionless car.

The wail of sirens sliced through the tense air, echoing off the vineyard rows as backup officers came in pursuit.

For now, though, they were isolated.

Nathan and Casey approached the vineyard manager's stalled vehicle.

Nathan's gun was in hand, and Casey wondered if she had to remind him not to *shoot* an unarmed suspect. No, no... he wouldn't, she knew that, but his glower suggested otherwise.

But Nathan flung open the door to the front of the car and was met by a trembling, thin face, and upraised, shaking hands.

"Don't shoot!" the voice said.

Somehow, he sounded even more slurred than before, and Casey noticed the two small bottles on the seat next to him.

Casey's heart sank as she realized that the vineyard manager was well and truly drunk. She exchanged a glance with Nathan.

"Sir, step out of the vehicle, please," Casey said firmly, her voice betraying her frustration.

The man stumbled out of the car, swaying unsteadily on his feet. Nathan stepped forward, his gun still trained on the suspect.

"I... It's all a big misunderstanding," Vincente said, hiccupping.

Nathan was already pushing him against the car, pulling his hands up behind his back.

Casey frowned, studying the man as he protested weakly, shaking his head.

"All just a misunderstanding!" he kept saying.

But he'd been seen at the crime scene the morning of the murder. He'd fled in his car when pressed by the FBI.

These were not the actions of an innocent man.

He was now drunk and shaking on his feet even as he was cuffed.

Nathan, in an impressive show of forearm strength, held the man upright from where he nearly stumbled.

Then, Nathan pushed the cuffed man towards their waiting car.

Casey frowned, but didn't follow.

She ducked inside the sports car, looking around.

There were more empty, small bottles discarded in the back seat. The entire car smelled of leather and alcohol. A thin layer of dust skimmed the upholstery.

She wrinkled her nose and opened the glove compartment.

She frowned, staring at a dark, black item sitting there.

She reached out, careful not to touch the item itself, but moving some papers so she could get a better look.

A gun.

Vincente had a gun in his car. She frowned, taking a photo of the item before pushing back out of the car and turning back to their own vehicle.

CHAPTER SEVEN

The cold, sterile light of the interrogation room cast a pale aura around Casey as she stepped inside, her footsteps echoing off the linoleum floor. Nathan followed closely behind her, his gaze shifting to their suspect.

Gabriel Vincente sat slumped in a chair, his disheveled appearance painting a picture of a man who had lost control. His unkempt hair hung in greasy strands around his face, and his once crisp white shirt was now stained with sweat and grime. The acrid smell of alcohol clung to the air like a malevolent specter, making it difficult for Casey to breathe. Her synesthetic senses recoiled at the onslaught.

Despite the gloves she wore, Casey's hands tingled, reacting to the textures she could have felt without them: the roughness of Gabriel's unshaven face, the dampness of his clothes.

Of course, she didn't make a habit of pawing at their suspects, but one's imagination was a strange thing.

She clenched her fists, focusing instead on the task at hand.

As Nathan moved to stand against the wall, Casey took her seat across from Gabriel, her eyes locked onto his. He seemed to shrink under her unwavering scrutiny.

Casey's gaze followed the nervous flicker of Gabriel's eyes as they darted around the room, seeking an escape route that didn't exist. His hands fidgeted with the edge of the table, the restless tapping and scraping of his fingers a symphony of unease. She could almost taste the metallic tang of his fear, a bitter note that lingered on her tongue.

"Mr. Vincente," Casey began, her voice a calm contrast to the storm raging within their suspect. "We need to discuss your relationship with Jamie Stevens."

At the mention of the victim's name, Gabriel's fidgeting intensified, but he managed to lift his eyes to meet hers. A glimmer of defiance flashed in their depths, only to be smothered by uncertainty.

"Look, I didn't know her," he said, his voice wavering like a flame buffeted by the wind.

With each word, Casey sensed the tendrils of anxiety wrapping themselves tighter around Gabriel's heart. The colors swirling in her mind sharpened, the dark blues and purples of deception intermingling with the sickly greens of guilt. She needed to press him further, to peel away the layers of his lies.

"Please, don't make this harder on yourself," Casey implored. "Tell us the truth, Gabriel. We need to understand what happened between you and Jamie."

Using the victim's name was intentional. She wanted to tug at whatever heartstrings might exist in Gabriel.

With a shuddering breath, he steeled himself, his jaw clenching.

"Never met her," he said simply.

"That's not what we hear," said Casey quietly. "We had her financials pulled. She was a guest at your vineyard a week ago."

He stared at her.

"We can check receipts, you know," she said softly.

The information alone was forceful enough; there was no reason to add to it.

He was already quailing.

The sterile silence of the interrogation room was broken only by the soft whirring of the overhead fan. Casey stared intently at Gabriel, her fingers tapping rhythmically on the table as she waited for him to answer. The scent of alcohol still lingered in the air, a stark reminder of his recent transgressions.

"Gabriel," Nathan interjected, his voice low and stern, "you need to start talking. The sooner you cooperate, the sooner we can sort this out."

Sweat beaded on Gabriel's forehead, his eyes darting nervously to the one-way mirror before returning to Casey's unwavering gaze. He swallowed hard, the sound audible in the hushed room, and finally began to speak.

"Alright," he started, his voice strained and hoarse. "I knew Jamie. But only barely."

"Is that why you ran?"

"I drove," he replied.

"Sarcasm isn't going to help here."

As the words left his mouth, Casey felt her synesthesia flare, a sudden rush of vibrant red flooding her vision like spilled ink. She blinked rapidly, trying to maintain focus as her mind swirled with the implications of the color, a visceral reminder of anger and betrayal.

"So why did you flee? Drive, as you say?"

Gabriel's jaw tightened, his hands balling into fists beneath the table. "You don't understand," he spat.

"Then help me understand," she pressed, her voice an icy whisper. "Help me see past the lies and the fear, Gabriel. Show me the truth."

Her pulse raced, adrenaline coursing through her veins as she scrutinized every subtle shift in his expression, every flicker of emotion that played across his features. It was a high-stakes game of intuition and observation, a dance between predator and prey that would determine the fate of both parties.

"Fine," he finally acquiesced, the word a defeated sigh. "I'll tell you everything. But you have to promise not to judge me."

"Judgment is not my prerogative," Casey assured him, though her thoughts were far from placid.

The room seemed to shrink around them, the sterile walls closing in as Casey leaned forward, her dark eyes never leaving Gabriel's face. She could feel Nathan's presence beside her, his steady energy grounding her as she prepared to delve deeper into the abyss of Gabriel's twisted story.

"Tell me more," Casey urged, her voice soft yet unyielding. "What happened between you and Jamie?"

Gabriel's hands trembled slightly, betraying the facade of indifference he had managed to attempt thus far. He hesitated, his gaze darting to the corners of the room as if searching for an escape.

"Alright," he sighed at last, a look of resignation on his disheveled face. "I... I tried to make a move on her. It was stupid, I know, but... I thought she liked me too."

As the words tumbled from his lips, Gabriel's eyes met Casey's, a flicker of vulnerability shining through the haze of guilt and shame. But it was short-lived, replaced almost immediately by a flare of anger that burned bright and hot in the depths of his soul.

"She laughed at me," he confessed, his voice tight with rage. "She told me I was pathetic, that she'd never be interested in someone like me. And then she just walked away like I was nothing."

Casey felt a shiver run down her spine, the intensity of his emotions resonating within her synesthetic perception like a discordant ensemble. She fought to keep her own feelings in check, knowing that she needed to remain objective if she was to uncover the whole truth.

"Gabriel, I understand that must have been hurtful for you," she said, her tone compassionate yet firm. "But how does that justify running from the police? There has to be more to this story."

Her instincts screamed at her. "Tell me the whole truth, Gabriel."

The sterile light of the interrogation room cast a harsh, unforgiving glow on Gabriel Vincente's face, revealing the cracks and crevices formed by a life of hardship and desperation. Casey sensed the weight of his secrets pressing down upon him like a suffocating fog, the vibrant hues of his fear and shame coalescing into a swirling vortex of color and texture that threatened to consume her own thoughts.

"Gabriel," she said, her voice steady despite the turmoil within her mind. "I understand that you were hurt and angry when Jamie rejected you. Did you lash out? Did you hurt her?"

She watched as Gabriel shifted uncomfortably in his chair, the cold steel cuff around his wrist chafing against his skin. His eyes darted nervously from side to side, the frayed edge of the table beneath his fingertips a testament to the mounting anxiety that gripped him like a vice.

"Look, I-I don't know what you want me to say," he stammered, sweat beading on his brow. "I panicked, alright? And now I'm here with you, trying to explain myself."

Casey glanced over at Nathan, who stood silently by the door, his keen gaze never leaving Gabriel's face. She knew that he too sensed that there was more to this story than met the eye.

One didn't flee the feds over unrequited love. Turning back to the suspect, Casey leaned in closer, her eyes boring into his with unyielding determination.

"Gabriel," she said softly, each syllable punctuated by a crisp beat of synesthetic color, "I can see that there's something you're not telling us. Something that has you terrified to your very core. But we can't help you unless you tell us the whole truth."

As she spoke, the room seemed to contract around them, the stark walls closing in like the relentless jaws of a predator. The air grew thick with tension, charged with the metallic taste of fear and the coarse, gritty texture of deceit. And as Gabriel Vincente's eyes flickered with a new wave of panic, Casey knew that she was on the cusp.

Casey's gloved fingers drummed against the cold metal table, her blue eyes narrowing in on Gabriel as she weighed the risks in her mind.

"Gabriel," Casey said, her voice calm but laced with authority. "I need you to understand the gravity of the situation you're in. We're not talking about just an altercation or a misunderstanding. If we find any evidence connecting you to Jamie's murder, you'll be facing life in prison – if you're lucky."

The color drained from Gabriel's face, leaving him ashen and vulnerable. His hands trembled, fingers clawing at the edge of the table as if it was his last lifeline.

"Murder," said Nathan, emphasizing the point. "You're our only suspect. Our lead suspect. I already have some of the paperwork drawn up--we're going to arrest you, Gabe."

He stared, stunned.

"Unless you give us a reason not to," said Casey.

The two agents stared at their suspect where he sat frozen in place, wide-eyed and horrified.

"Please," Gabriel choked out, tears streaming down his cheeks. "I didn't – I didn't kill her. But... there's something I haven't told you." He said this last part with desperation in his voice, as if seeking their approval.

"Go on," Casey encouraged, locking eyes with him. She tasted the bitterness of desperation on her tongue.

"A few weeks ago," he began, his voice barely audible, but picking up volume and speed as he spoke, "I tried to drug Jamie. I wanted her to like me, to give me a chance. But it didn't work, and she figured it out. She was so angry, so disgusted. She threatened to expose me, ruin my life. That's why I ran when the police showed up. I was scared, but I swear, I didn't kill her."

"You tried to roofie her?"

"What? No! No… just to get high together. To relax. I thought it'd be fun."

"Thank you for telling us, Gabriel," she said softly, trying to quell the emotions inside her. "We'll need to verify your story, of course. And trying to drug someone is a serious offense. But if what you're saying is true, it might help us find the real killer."

"Jamie... she found out," Gabriel choked out, his voice barely audible above the hum of the fluorescent lights. "She confronted me about it, said she'd tell everyone what I did if I didn't leave her alone."

His hands trembled on the table as he spoke, his eyes darting between Casey and Nathan, seeking some semblance of understanding, or perhaps absolution. Casey clenched her gloved fists at her side, her heart pounding in her ears like a tribal drum, urging her to press on, to pry open the secrets that still lay hidden beneath the surface of Gabriel's confession.

"Did you ever approach her again after she threatened to expose your actions?" Casey asked, her voice cold, betraying none of the empathy she felt for the victim.

"Never," Gabriel whispered, averting his gaze. "I was too ashamed of what I'd done and scared of what would happen if she told."

Casey studied him intently, noting the way his shoulders sagged, the weight of his guilt pressing down upon him with every word. And yet, there remained a flicker of doubt within her, a nagging suspicion fueled by the vibrant colors and textures her synesthesia painted in her mind.

"Then why run from the police, Gabriel?" Casey probed, her thoughts racing like a bloodhound on the scent. "If you truly had no connection to Jamie's death, why flee?"

"Because..." Gabriel hesitated, swallowing hard before continuing. "Because I knew how it would look. I knew they'd find out about my attempt to drug her and think I'd killed her to keep her quiet."

He looked up at Casey, and she could see the raw fear in his eyes. The red of anger had faded, replaced with an array of blues and grays that spoke of sadness and desperation.

"Please," Gabriel implored, tears streaming down his face. "I know what I did was wrong, but I didn't kill Jamie. I swear it."

Casey's chest tightened, as if bound by invisible ropes, constricting her breath and clouding her thoughts. She knew she couldn't afford to let her emotions rule her judgment – not when lives hung in the balance, and a killer still roamed free.

"Gabriel," Casey began in a measured tone, her dark eyes locked onto his, "I need you to provide proof of your alibi for the night Jamie was murdered."

A shudder ran through Gabriel's disheveled form, like a chill wind whispering through an abandoned building. His eyes, once darting nervously, now bore into hers with a desperation that made her stomach twist.

"Please," he pleaded, his voice cracking under the weight of his fear. "You have to believe me. I didn't kill her. I wasn't even there."

Casey leaned forward in her chair, her hands folded neatly on the cold metal table that separated them.

"I..." suddenly his eyes widened.

"What is it?" she said sharply.

He just stared at her, mouth agape. "I was at my office."

"Excuse me?"

"I was there this morning, early, because I was at the office. The entire time. And then I left."

"Can you prove it?"

"Yes!" he said emphatically. "There's a camera in my office. "It'll show me there, sitting at the desk. That's it."

"Why were you there."

"Finishing up some of the books from last night." He shrugged. "It was a busy night."

"And the cameras won't show you ever leaving your office?"

"Only through the side door--it leads directly to the parking lot. I was *never* near the vats." He said this part triumphantly, and his eyes held a flicker of relief.

She stared at him, but he didn't look away.

"We're going to need access to the security footage."

"Done," he said reflexively.

She shared a look with Nathan. He was frowning, too. Neither of them liked the eager note to Vincente's voice. As if he *wanted* them to check out his alibi.

But only an innocent party's alibi would be ironclad.

Innocent of murder.

He was still slimy--he'd tried to drug the woman. He'd lied, and then he'd fled the cops.

But if he was telling the truth, and if the cameras proved it, he hadn't killed anyone.

"I can give you my password right now," he said. "The footage can be accessed from my phone."

Casey felt a creeping sense of doubt. She extended her hand.

"Alright. Let's have it, then."

CHAPTER EIGHT

She drove fast, indifferent to the fear of collision.

Claire's adrenaline spiked as she veered one way then the other.

The inky darkness enveloped the narrow road, snaking through the countryside like a sinister ribbon. Shadows cast by twisted branches stretched across the pavement, their forms distorted and elongated by the pale glow of the moon overhead. A faint breeze rustled the leaves of the vineyard to one side, their vines heavy with ripe grapes that gleamed like amethysts under the silvery light. The other side of the road was bordered by a dense thicket, its tangled underbrush impenetrable even to the keenest eye. This was not a place for the weary or the faint of heart.

Claire gripped the steering wheel tightly, her knuckles turning white as she navigated the treacherous curves. Her senses were heightened, every sound amplified – the crunch of gravel beneath the tires, the hum of the car engine, even her own breathing seemed deafeningly loud. She glanced at the empty passenger seat beside her, wondering for the umpteenth time if she should have accepted her boyfriend's offer to accompany her after the wine-tasting event. It wasn't that she had consumed an excessive amount of alcohol – in fact, she had been uncharacteristically cautious, sipping each variety slowly and methodically, careful not to let the intoxicating flavors cloud her judgment.

But the effects of the wine were still present, swirling through her bloodstream and casting a gossamer veil over her thoughts.

"Focus," she whispered to herself, blinking rapidly to dispel the tendrils of fog that threatened to obscure her vision. This was no time for distraction or hesitation, not when the shadows along the roadside seemed to pulse with malevolent energy. Claire could feel her vulnerability, knew that the combination of darkness, isolation, and the remnants of the wine had left her susceptible to the dangers that lurked within the night.

And that's when she spotted him.

Like a wraith, emerging from the mist.

The man on the side of the road was a stark contrast to the inky darkness surrounding him, his white shirt catching the faint moonlight as he stood there, one arm outstretched and the other clutching at his chest. He appeared distraught, his handsome face twisted in anguish, brows furrowed and eyes shimmering with unshed tears that threatened to spill down his cheeks. His wavy dark hair fell in disarray around his forehead, adding an air of vulnerability to his otherwise strong features. She slowed as she turned the switchback, forced to a lower speed. Claire's curiosity piqued, her heart rate accelerating, not entirely from fear but also from intrigue.

As she slowed the car to a crawl, the engine hummed softly, almost imperceptibly, beneath the haunting melody of the night breeze rustling through the vineyard leaves. The lingering taste of wine still coated her tongue, a mixture of earthy tannins and sweet fruitiness.

"Hey," she called out through the crack of her window. "Are you okay?"

The man's gaze snapped to Claire's car, his eyes wide and wild with desperation. "I –" he stammered, swallowing hard as he struggled to find his voice. Tears were visible in his mesmerizing eyes--he *really* was quite handsome.

The man approached her idling car, each hesitant step sending a new shiver down her spine.

"Please," he choked out through tear-streaked cheeks, "I need help."

"What happened?" Claire asked, forcing herself to maintain eye contact with the stranger. The shadows from the vineyard danced across his face, accentuating his chiseled features.

"I –" His voice wavered, raw with emotion. "I can't... I just can't say it."

"Can you at least tell me your name?" Claire ventured, attempting to ground the conversation in reality.

"Adam," he replied, his voice barely audible over the rustling leaves and distant hoot of an owl. Claire noticed his hands trembling as he wiped away a fresh trickle of tears.

"God, I didn't mean for it to happen." He closed his eyes for a moment, taking a deep breath. "It was an accident, but I –" He broke off abruptly, chest heaving as he struggled to regain control of his emotions.

"An accident?" Claire echoed, her mind racing to fill in the blanks. Her fingers drummed against the steering wheel in time with her pounding heart. Every instinct told her to flee, but the desperation in Adam's eyes held her captive.

41

"Please," he begged again, his voice cracking.

Claire's heart pounded harder, mimicking the rhythm of her anxious thoughts. What kind of accident could reduce a man to this state? She could feel her palms growing clammy against the smooth leather of the steering wheel, her breaths shallow and uneven.

"Adam," she began, trying to keep her voice steady, "I want to help you, really, I do. But I need more information. What happened?"

His gaze darted away for a split second before returning to meet hers. Claire couldn't help but notice how his eyes seemed to flicker with an inner turmoil, like a storm brewing just beneath the surface.

"Someone... someone got hurt," he confessed, each word laced with guilt and pain. "I didn't mean for it to happen."

"Who?" Claire asked hesitantly, feeling a knot tightening in the pit of her stomach.

"Her name is..." he swallowed hard, his Adam's apple bobbing nervously.

"I... I need to go," Claire said suddenly. He was standing much closer. When had that happened?

She found herself staring at his handsome, tear-streaked features.

Claire's head swam with questions, but before she could ask another, Adam's hand shot through the open window with an unexpected swiftness. Her breath caught in her throat as his fingers closed around her keys, wrenching them from the ignition.

"Hey!" she protested, panic surging through her veins. "What are you doing?"

"Forgive me," he whispered, his voice suddenly edged with steel. "But I can't let you leave."

In a split second, Claire's heart pounded in her chest like a wild animal, desperate to break free from its cage. She drew in a shaky breath, trying to muster the courage to scream for help. But as her lips parted, no sound emerged – only a strangled gasp.

"Please," she whispered, the word barely audible. Her eyes locked onto his, searching for some remnant of humanity, something to cling to amidst the darkness that seemed to be swallowing him whole. "Don't hurt me."

"I never meant for this," Adam choked out, tears streaming down his face. His grip on her keys tightened, knuckles white as the moonlight that filtered through the trees overhead. "I'm so sorry."

Claire's mind raced, a chaotic whirlwind of fear and confusion.

His eyes flickered with uncertainty for just a moment before the stormy clouds of desperation rolled back in, eclipsing any hope that had

42

dared to emerge. And then, without warning, his hand shot out, fingers wrapping around her throat with an iron grip.

CHAPTER NINE

Casey scowled at the computer as she studied the footage they'd transferred from Vincente's phone.

He'd been telling the truth.

The vineyard manager had stayed in his office, then left.

She massaged the bridge of her nose as she played the video for what felt like the tenth time.

Small earbuds resounded with cello music in her ears. She found the sound quite soothing, and it helped her focus. The gloves were removed now, allowing her fingertips to feel the cold of the keyboard.

She watched the screen as Vincente sat at his computer, moved about the office a bit, then left.

He'd never once ventured into the room with the vats.

There was no sign of the victim.

"So if not you, then who?" she whispered.

She slumped in her chair, closing her eyes briefly. When she opened them again, she loosed a long exhale.

The small office room she'd borrowed felt more like a closet than anything else.

Casey began to wonder if she was looking in the wrong place. Vincente seemed like the most likely suspect, but the footage showed no evidence of him being involved in Stevens' death. She leaned back in her chair and rubbed her temples, trying to think of other possibilities.

As she closed her eyes, the cello music became more prominent in her mind. She let herself get lost in the melody, feeling the notes wrap around her like a comforting blanket.

A woman had been drowned in a vat of wine.

It was so macabre, like something out of a mystery story.

She frowned, shaking her head.

What if she was making this too complicated?

She frowned, sitting upright now, staring at her computer. She closed the window with the security footage, and bit her lower lip.

The faint pain helped her focus.

"Let's see..." she muttered to herself.

She typed into the search bar of the web browser, *Drowned in vat.*

She scanned the articles. A surprising number, but none local.

She tried again. *Drowned in wine. Seattle.*

She stared.

Two results.

They were lower down the page, but they caught her attention almost immediately.

She stared at the titles of the two articles.

Woman drowned in tub full of grape juice.

Woman chokes on Merlot.

She stared at the bizarre headlines.

One from two years ago and another in the same time frame, but only a week after.

As she read through the articles, Casey's heart raced. The similarities between the cases were too much to ignore. Both women were found dead in wine-related incidents, and while both deaths were initially ruled as accidents, upon closer investigation, it was discovered that foul play was involved in both cases.

Casey leaned back in her chair, deep in thought. Could it be possible that the death of Stevens was connected to these other cases? It was a long shot, but it was worth looking into.

And what better place to start than the victims?

Alone, Jamie Stevens was a single data point. But with the possibility of two other cases?

She re-read through the files. Both other women had also drowned.

If she looked into all three... maybe they'd have a connecting point.

She nodded resolutely. She reached out, pulling on her gloves, slowly, aware that she'd be typing for quite some time.

The dimly lit office felt like a cave, shrouded in shadows. Casey sat at the cluttered desk, her focused eyes trained on the computer screen before her. The glow of the screen illuminated her face, casting an eerie light on her sharp features. Stacks of files surrounded her like ancient relics.

As she delved into the records, her synesthetic experience came alive. Words transformed into colors that danced and swirled around her, while numbers twisted themselves into intricate patterns. Each fact she uncovered seemed to have its own unique hue and texture, creating an abstract tapestry within her mind. The colors and textures weren't just visual; they carried a weight, a sensation that she could feel brushing against her consciousness. It was as if her gloves were not enough to protect her from the flood of sensations that threatened to overwhelm her.

"Stevens... Fisher... Ko," she muttered to herself, forcing her thoughts to focus on the three women whose lives had inexplicably intertwined. She could see their names shimmering like ghostly apparitions, shifting between shades of blue, green, and red - each one a puzzle waiting to be solved.

With every new database she accessed, Casey's determination grew. She meticulously cross-referenced their backgrounds, searching for hidden connections that might reveal the key to unlocking the mystery that bound them together. Her fingers flew across the keyboard, leaving a trail of color in their wake as she navigated through layers upon layers of information.

But as the time wore on, her initial excitement began to wane. The vibrant hues of discovery slowly dulled into a murky gray, tinged with frustration and doubt. Small details that once promised to be the missing pieces to the puzzle now led only to dead ends, leaving her more lost than before.

"Come on, Casey," she muttered to herself, steeling her resolve. "There must be something here."

Casey dragged her gloved hands through her dark hair, feeling the tension in her scalp as she pulled it back into a tighter ponytail. The sensation was grounding, a momentary reprieve from the sea of colors that swirled in her mind with every new document she read. She sighed heavily.

"Jamie Stevens, Mary Fisher, Julia Ko," she whispered the names to herself, hoping that saying them aloud would somehow make their connections clearer. But the air around her remained stubbornly opaque, refusing to reveal anything.

She stared at the computer screen, willing it to show her something she had missed, some overlooked detail that would finally bring these disparate lives together and offer an answer to the question that haunted her: DMV files, school records, medical payments... None of them tied the women together.

Her frustration mounted as she clicked through countless records, each one more frustratingly unconnected than the last.

"Nothing... absolutely nothing," she muttered under her breath, barely suppressing the urge to slam her fists on the desk. "Three drowned women, and not a single link between them."

And then, just as the last vestiges of hope threatened to slip through her fingers, she stumbled upon a seemingly insignificant piece of information – a single post on social media that all three women had liked.

She double-checked. But the keyword appeared in each of the social profiles. It was a tenuous connection at best, but it was something – a fragile thread.

She stared at the screen, frowning.

A craft show.

The social media profile advertised a local craft show.

She double-checked the graphic, and then the comments below.

It had taken place nearly three years ago.

Was that too much of a stretch?

She studied the image on the screen of the craft show flyer.

Slowly, she pushed to her feet, grabbing her jacket from over the chair.

She paused, considering her options. There was a number on the flyer. Three years ago...

But that didn't mean the show wouldn't continue. It had been on Tuesdays, Wednesdays and Saturdays.

And today was Wednesday.

She dialed the number on the flyer, fingers crossed in her gloves.

As she waited for the call to connect, Casey's heart pounded in her chest. What if this was a dead end, too? What if she was chasing shadows and ghosts that didn't exist? But then, just as she was about to give up hope, a voice answered on the other end of the line.

"Hello?" it said, sounding tentative and unsure.

"Hi, my name is Casey, and I'm calling about the Cringle Market that took place three years ago. I was wondering if you still host it?" Her voice was steady, but inside she felt like a ball of nerves, waiting for the answer that could make or break the case.

There was a pause on the other end, and then a hesitant voice replied. "Yes, we do still have it. It's on Wednesdays and Saturdays, from ten in the morning until two in the afternoon. Can I help you with anything else?"

Casey felt a thrill of excitement run through her. "Yes, actually. I was wondering if you could tell me if there were any vendors or attendees who had a connection to three women."

"Umm... Who?"

"Their names are Mary Fisher, Julia Ko, or Jamie Stevens."

The person on the other end was silent for a moment, and Casey held her breath, waiting for a response. Finally, they spoke. "I'm not sure, but I can ask around and see if anyone remembers them. Can I get your number in case I find anything?"

Casey rattled off her number, her heart racing with anticipation.

"It might take me some time. We're open today, actually."

"Right..." Casey paused. "What do you sell at the show?"

"Oh, all sorts of things."

"Like?"

"Well, we have handmade jewelry, pottery, candles, and a lot of other crafts. It's a pretty big market, so there are a lot of different vendors."

Casey nodded to herself, taking in the information. "Thank you. That's helpful. I'll be there today, actually. Just in case anyone remembers anything."

"Sure thing. Is there a specific vendor you're interested in?"

Casey hesitated. But she decided to keep her business to herself.

"No. No, that's fine. Is it still at the same address?"

"Grace Lutheran Church," the voice replied. "Same as always. We look forward to having you with us!"

Casey hung up the phone, a sense of purpose driving her forward. She grabbed her keys and headed out the door, her mind already racing with possibilities.

What would a craftshow have in common that would've led to the deaths of three women?

Was she grasping at straws?

Perhaps.

But there was nothing else *to* grasp at.

She nodded to herself, feeling a rising sense of excitement.

Down the hall, she spotted Nathan Hayes leaning against a soda machine, puffing on a vape pen.

He'd quit smoking a while ago, but had never put down the pen.

As he blew a plume of water vapor in the air, she detected the scent of strawberries.

"I might have a lead," she said to her partner.

He scratched at his stubble, eyeing her.

"The security footage?"

"No," she said quickly. "Checks out. Not him."

A blink. "That was quick."

"He's on it the entire time, like he said. Never enters the front door. Never heads to the back room."

"Shit."

She nodded.

He stowed his pen. "So what's this news?"

She brightened. "A craft show."

"Er... what?"

"Come on!" she called over her shoulder, already hurrying towards the door.

"No, wait--hang on, Ms. Cryptic. Where are we going?"

She paused, turning back to look at her partner. They both faced one another, and she noticed the way his hand hovered near her arm, rather than touching it.

A considerate gesture; he knew that sudden, unexpected physical contact could sometimes play havoc with her senses.

She patted him on the back of his hand with her gloved fingers, then said, "All three victims liked a craft show post from three years ago."

"Hang on. *Three* victims? What *three*?"

"Oh, didn't I tell you?"

"No."

"Two other women drowned as well. Now let's go!"

She pushed out the front door without looking back.

CHAPTER TEN

The Seattle craft show buzzed with life, a throng of people weaving through rows of booths that stretched as far as the eye could see.

Casey stared at the spectacle; when she'd read about the craft show online, she hadn't been expecting something *this* large. It filled out the entirety of an abandoned glass-roof train station.

The booths were a sight to behold. Each one was unique, with its own design and atmosphere. Some had bright colors, decorations, and items spilling out of them. Others were more subdued, their owners preferring to focus on the intricacies of the crafts they sold rather than flashy displays. There was something for everyone: jewelry stands glittered in the sunbeams that filtered through the glass roof, while woodworkers displayed their intricate carvings and furniture makers proudly showed off their creations.

The air was full of delightful aromas – fresh-baked breads from the bakers, herbs from the herb merchants, and a variety of other scents that enticed Casey's nose as she wandered around. Everywhere she looked, there were people chatting and laughing as they examined different wares or discussed potential purchases with vendors.

Casey glanced at one booth in particular – a small jewelry stand run by an elderly woman who worked with silver and copper to create beautiful pieces of wearable art. She watched as the woman carefully displayed each piece with her steady hands, her face illuminated by a smile when someone admired her work or purchased one of her items.

Amidst this slew of colors and textures, Casey felt alive, her synesthesia heightening her senses in ways she couldn't quite describe.

"Look at this, Nathan," Casey said, gesturing toward an intricate wood carving of a vine, the twisting tendrils rendered with exquisite detail. She traced its contours with her gloved fingertips, reveling in the smooth texture beneath her touch.

Agent Nathan Hayes leaned in to examine it further, his salt-and-pepper hair glinting in the light. "That's amazing work," he agreed, clearly impressed. "I can't even imagine how much time and effort went into creating something like that."

Together, they wandered through the maze of exhibits, pausing to admire delicate pottery painted with rich hues. The flickering light from a nearby candle booth cast dancing shadows on the walls, adding a sense of warmth and intimacy to their surroundings.

Casey's gaze zeroed in on one booth in particular.

An artist's studio carrying all sort of sundry items and tchotchkes.

It wasn't the items themselves, but the subject matter that caught her attention.

Casey stared. Nathan followed her gaze.

And he paused, too.

This particular small stall was full of wine-tasting items. Ranging from wines from different countries to exquisite crystal glasses to intricate corkscrews.

Casey approached and ran her fingers over the bottles, feeling the texture of their labels and the weight of the glass as she picked them up to examine them more closely.

Three women drowned in wine-related incidents.

All three had liked a post on a social media profile that had directed them here...

Coincidence?

It was hard to know.

"Excuse me," a voice called out, pulling Casey from her reverie. Turning, she saw a middle-aged woman approaching them from around the stall, her warm smile framed by laugh lines and golden-brown curls. She wore a flowing dress adorned with grapevine patterns, perfectly embodying the event's theme.

"Hello," Nathan greeted the woman, his voice friendly and curious. "Are you the artist behind these beautiful pieces?"

"Indeed, I am," the woman replied, her brown eyes twinkling with pride. "My name is Eleanor, and I've been creating wine-themed jewelry for years. It's become quite popular at these events."

"Your work is stunning," Casey complimented, her gaze returning to the table laden with treasures.

"Thank you," Eleanor responded, her cheeks flushing with pleasure. "I truly appreciate the kind words. There are so many incredible artisans here, it's an honor to be counted among them."

"Speaking of other artisans," Casey began tentatively, "Are you the only one who does wine-themed pieces?"

"Oh, umm, no. There was another one. He was more of a woodworker, really."

"And what was his name?"

Eleanor's face clouded.

"I'm not looking to buy from him," Casey said quickly. "Just curious."

"Ah, yes. His name is Robert, and he was quite the talent. It's a shame he hasn't been around lately – his work was always a favorite among the attendees. Last I heard, he had taken some time off for personal reasons, but no one seems to know much more than that."

Nathan nodded slowly. He said, "Do you know the names Jamie Stevens, Mary Fisher or Julia Ko?"

The woman looked puzzled and shook her head. "No... should I? Are they here too?"

Casey examined the woman. She had a pleasant disposition, and her posture and attitude was causing a faint warmth to spread over her skin.

Not everyone's synesthesia combined both visual and auditory with physical, but hers was a very rare sort, and now she had the calming sensation that the woman was at ease.

Puzzled, but not guilty.

Besides, she was far too frail to have lifted anyone and shoved them in a vat of wine.

"Do you tend this stall alone?"

"Y-yes...My son sometimes helps."

"Where's he?"

"At school. He's twelve."

Casey glanced at Nathan.

"Is there a man in the picture?"

"Umm... no. Not for years now. May I ask why all these questions?"

But Casey was already shaking her head apologetically. "So sorry-- we don't mean to pry. But this man, this other wine artisan. What was his last name? Robert what?"

"Darlo, I think. Robert Darlo."

"What was your sense of him, on a personal level?"

"He was a great craftsman."

"But what about him as a person?"

"I wouldn't know."

Casey nodded. "Didn't spend much time speaking with him?"

"No..." The artisan hesitated now, wrinkling her nose. "Are you police?"

"Something like that," Nathan said. "So if you didn't know him, what was the general impression of Robert?"

"I... did he do something?"

Casey wasn't sure how they could answer this question. The only guilt the man had was of creating wine-inspired art at a craft fair liked by three victims.

None of that tied him to the murders...

But the coincidences were mounting up.

"Robert was well-liked," she said hesitantly. And then she paused, frowning.

"That," Nathan said sharply. "What did you just remember?"

"Oh... umm..." She hesitated, wincing. "There was a small incident. A few weeks ago."

"What sort of incident?"

Eleanor shifted her weight from one foot to the other, looking uncomfortable. "It was nothing, really. Just a disagreement between Robert and another vendor. They got into a shouting match over something, and Robert stormed off. I haven't seen him since."

Nathan and Casey exchanged a glance. "Do you remember the other vendor's name?" Nathan asked.

Eleanor shook her head. "I'm sorry, I don't. But I know he's not here today."

"Do you know why not?"

She hesitated. "I'm not one to gossip..."

"But?" Casey pressed.

"But... I think Robert may have made a comment about the other vendor's wife, and he wanted nothing to do with him after that."

Nathan and Casey shared another look. They offered their thanks before turning and beginning to move one again away from the booth.

Casey hesitated, then held up a finger. She pulled out her wallet, hastened back and purchased two of the custom corks.

Then, fidgeting with the items in her pocket, she returned to where Nathan was waiting by a tall, concrete pillar.

"Let's find a quiet corner so we can look into this Robert guy," she suggested to Nathan, her voice low.

"Agreed," he replied. "The wine iconography. Seems like a big stretch to just be a coincidence."

"Mhmm."

They found respite in an alcove near a booth displaying hand-painted candle jars, where the colors danced across the glass. Casey pulled out her phone and searched for any information she could find on Robert Darlo.

But there was nothing local. She frowned, trying the search again with different spelling.

53

"Nothing," she said.

"Hang on," Nathan replied quickly.

She glanced over.

His eyebrows were high on his forehead, and his dark eyes fixated on the screen in hand. "Shit," he said. "Here's why."

He turned his phone so she could see it. *Robert Darlo. Incarcerated 2013.*

She blinked. "Incarcerated?"

"Yeah. Robert Darlo is still in prison."

"So... who's our craft fair attendee? I mean... maybe it's just a coincidence they have the same name."

"You really think that?"

"I think we need to speak to the event coordinator and get an address for our missing vendor."

CHAPTER ELEVEN

Casey found the small offices in a row of paneled rooms at the back of the event.

The only door marked had a nameplate which read, *Jacinda Fowler, Coordinator.*

Casey knocked, but received no reply, so she pushed open the door to spot a figure hunched behind a small desk.

The event coordinator, a middle-aged woman with frazzled, disheveled hair, sat behind a desk cluttered with overdue paperwork. Her smile faltered under the weight of her worry, which clouded her eyes as she searched for the right form. The craft show hummed with activity behind them, but this small space seemed to hold it all at bay.

"Excuse me," Casey called out, her voice calm but assertive. She observed the coordinator's hands fluttering nervously through the stacks of documents as if they were trying to find their way in a maze.

"Can I help you?" the coordinator asked, her eyes darting up to meet Casey's gaze before retreating back to the chaos of her desk.

Casey briefly exchanged glances with Nathan, whose presence seemed to fill the cramped room. His tattooed knuckles rested on the edge of the doorway, the word "Bless" spelled out across them like a reminder of his tough upbringing. With a swift motion, Casey unclipped her FBI badge from her waistband and held it up for the coordinator to see.

"Special Agent Casey Bolt," she announced, her tone firm. "This is Agent Nathan Hayes. We need information about one of your vendors."

The coordinator's demeanor shifted immediately, her pleasant smile vanishing as she stared at Casey's badge. The way her eyes widened betrayed her nervousness, and her lips pressed into a thin line. She glanced over at Nathan.

"Of course," she stammered, trying to regain her composure. "Please, have a seat."

As Casey and Nathan took their seats, the coordinator looked from one to the other, her fingers fidgeting with the pen in her hand. She could sense the gravity of the situation, and the air in the room grew heavy with unspoken tension.

"Tell us about Robert Darlo," Casey said, her voice steady but laced with urgency. She knew that time was of the essence, and she needed to extract every possible lead from this conversation.

The coordinator hesitated, avoiding eye contact as she fumbled with her paperwork. It was clear that she was fearful, but whether it was fear for herself or reluctance to reveal information about Darlo remained uncertain.

"Mr. Dralo is a vendor here at the fairgrounds," she began cautiously, her voice trembling slightly. "I can't say much more than that."

"Ma'am, we need to find him as soon as possible," Nathan emphasized, his own impatience simmering beneath his gruff tone.

"Robert... I hardly know anything about him. He was just a vendor here at the fair," the coordinator stammered, her voice now a frayed ribbon of azure.

The scent of fear wafted from her, a bitterness that coiled around Casey's senses like tendrils of smoke.

The coordinator's hands trembled as she clutched the stack of papers to her chest, her knuckles turning white under the pressure. She appeared lost in an internal struggle, her eyes flicking back and forth between Casey and Nathan. The fear that emanated from her was a bitter taste on Casey's tongue, a dark cloud hovering over them all.

"Was?" Casey said, remembering what they'd been told already. "So he's no longer a vendor?"

"No," she said firmly.

"Why not?"

"Is... did someone complain?"

"We heard about the altercation," Nathan said.

She glanced at him. "Oh? So you already know?"

"We want to hear it from you. What happened, exactly?"

She fidgeted uncomfortably and sighed. "We run a legal business here, mind you. It's for artists. It's not... not meant for ruffians." She grimaced.

"So?" Nathan pressed. "What was the altercation over?"

"Another vendor's wife." She tensed. "Apparently, Robert Darlo made comments, or a pass at her. I'm told no physical interaction took place, but it made the women immensely uncomfortable."

She rattled this off, a flush to her face. She said, "I... I don't feel it necessary to get the FBI involved. I don't want to cause any trouble."

"You're not," Casey assured her. "Can you walk us through when this happened?"

"Last week."

"And what exactly transpired."

"What I've already said."

"I mean in detail. Please, if you don't mind." Casey rested her fingers on her badge once more.

The coordinator let out a sigh and leaned back in her chair, the sound of the creaking wood filling the small office. "It was during the set-up day for the fair. Robert and another vendor, Sam, were setting up their booths next to each other. Sam's wife, Karen, was helping him out. According to Karen, Robert made some inappropriate comments and gestures towards her. She felt uncomfortable and immediately told her husband. Sam confronted Robert, and things got heated. There was a lot of yelling and pushing, but someone eventually broke it up and the police were called. Robert was escorted off the premises and banned from participating in the fair. And Robert had..." She paused, biting her lip.

"What is it?" Nathan said.

"N-nothing... just... I didn't know at the time I allowed him."

"Know what?" Casey said. She could see the fear in the woman's eyes and the way she was holding back, as if there was something she wasn't revealing.

"Is there something else you're not telling us?" Casey asked, her tone gentle but probing.

The coordinator hesitated, her eyes flicking back and forth between the two agents. "I... I don't know if it's relevant, but there were rumors going around that Robert had a history of violence. Nothing concrete, just whispers. And I didn't know when I first leased him space here."

"Violence?" Nathan repeated, his voice low and dangerous. "What kind of violence?"

"I... I don't know," the coordinator stammered. "Just rumors. I didn't want to believe them, but..." She trailed off, her eyes fixed on some distant point behind Casey and Nathan.

"Alright... Do you have an address for Mr. Darlo?"

"I don't think I can give that without a warrant," she said hesitantly.

Casey paused, considering this, but decided she didn't have the time to play nice.

The red tape would only hamper the investigation at this point.

"Look," Casey said, her voice firm and resolute, "we don't want to cause any trouble for you or this fair. But if you don't cooperate, we may have no choice but to shut it down until we find Darlo."

Nathan chimed in, his tone equally as decisive. "We're not asking for much, just an address. If you help us now, you'll be saving yourself a lot more trouble later."

The coordinator's face blanched at their words, her breathing becoming labored as she weighed her options. Casey could feel the thrum of tension in the air, the colors of the scene around her vibrating with anticipation. The blues of the coordinator's voice now mingled with the steely grays of determination that radiated from both her and Nathan.

"Please," Casey whispered, the silver threads of her plea weaving through the cacophony of colors. "We need your help."

The coordinator swallowed hard, her gaze darting to the floor as she fidgeted nervously, the once vibrant blue of her voice now dissipating into a muted haze of uncertainty. It was clear that she was afraid, either of what might happen to her if she revealed the information or the repercussions should she withhold it.

"Alright," she finally muttered, her voice barely audible as she shuffled through the papers in her hands, searching for the address they sought. "But please, leave me out of this. I don't want any trouble. Here," she whispered, her voice barely audible as it fractured into a million shimmering fragments of blue and green, each one flickering with fear and resignation. She had pulled a piece of paper from a stack at her elbow, paused, then exchanged it for another and nodded. "This is the address where I sent the checks."

Casey reached out to take the paper, her gloved fingers brushing against the coordinator's trembling hand. The sensation was muted but still sent shivers down her spine; colors swirled around them, blending and separating like oil on water.

"Thank you," Casey said, her voice softening as she pocketed the address. "We appreciate your cooperation." She caught Nathan's eye, his gaze a swirling storm of gray determination and deep blue concern.

He was shaking his head in frustration. He sometimes got antsy when it felt as if they were going in circles.

He was very much a man of action rather than words.

As they left the office, she reached out, touching his arm. "Are you okay?" she said.

He shot her a look. "Asshole preys on women."

"Yeah."

He scratched at the side of his jaw. "It just reminds me..."

"Of what?"

"Stuff. Whatever. Not important. A different case. Long ago." He sighed, releasing a pent-up breath. "Let's go find this asshole."

He led the way back through the craft fair, the two of them weaving hurriedly through the milling throng of customers and hastening out the front doors towards where they had parked their car.

Casey glanced down at the address, frowning.

Darlo, R.

No one by that name lived at the address given. Not officially.

So why had he given a fake name?

Who was Robert Darlo?

CHAPTER TWELVE

The late afternoon sun cast long shadows on the empty house as Casey and Nathan climbed the steps to the front door. Wind whispered through the trees, rustling the leaves like an impatient audience waiting for a show to begin. Casey's gloved hands tightened around her FBI badge, her thoughts focused and sharp.

"Looks abandoned," Nathan remarked, glancing around at the peeling paint and overgrown weeds. "You sure this is the place?"

"Positive," Casey replied, adjusting the ponytail that kept her dark hair out of her face.

Nathan glanced around the place, his eyes narrowed as if in suspicion. He kept glancing over his shoulder, along the side of the alley, as if searching for lookouts. Her partner had grown up in rougher circumstances than most, and sometimes, in tense moments, his caution was visible.

But it was caution on behalf of others, more often than not.

He wasn't checking *his* back. He was watching hers.

And so once he'd decided they were safe, he didn't hesitate to step in front of her and enter the house.

Nathan pushed open the unlocked door, and they stepped inside, their shoes crunching on broken glass. The room was stripped bare, save for a few discarded items scattered across the floor. Casey scanned the desolate scene, her eyes searching for any clues that might lead them closer to their target.

"No one has lived here in a while," said Casey.

"Darlo has a fake name and a fake address," replied Nathan.

Casey just nodded. She ran her gloved finger over a trail of dust on the windowsill.

Then, she glanced back towards where Nathan was leaning over a trashcan, frowning.

"Still gets mail, though," Nathan murmured. "Look at this," he said, holding up a crumpled flier he had pulled from a trashcan in the corner. "An art auction, tonight. Seems like our kind of party."

"Maybe," Casey agreed, tucking the flier into her pocket. She knew better than to dismiss anything as coincidence. As Nathan continued to search the room, Casey caught a faint whiff of cologne, barely noticeable above the musty scent of abandonment.

"Wait," she murmured, her voice barely audible above the creaking floorboards. The scent triggered a synesthetic response, painting her mind with a vibrant red hue. It reminded her of something, someone, but she couldn't quite put her finger on it. "I know this cologne," she said, more to herself than Nathan.

"Who?" Nathan asked, his salt-and-pepper fringe catching the fading light as he turned to face her.

"Can't be sure," Casey admitted, her thoughts racing like the wind outside. She thought of Dr. Evelyn Reed briefly, her old mentor. A dear friend. It was a strange, jarring distraction--sometimes, the crosswiring of her senses could conjure such memories.

Casey looked around the space a bit more and then glanced down at the flyer Nathan had found.

"Hey," she murmured. "Look."

He leaned in. There, stuck to the side of the flyer, was a small form.

"Leroy Darlo?" she said.

"Using the same last name."

"But another fake first one," she said.

"What's the form for?"

Casey read the heading of the form, and her eyebrows lifted. "Oh..."

"What?"

"Looks like he's going to the art auction as a buyer..."

"A fake name... and now posing as an art purveyor? What's this guy up to?"

"Let's head to that art auction," Casey decided, her voice determined. "Maybe we'll find more than just expensive paintings."

"Sounds like a plan."

***

Exiting their car and taking the marble steps outside the art studio two at a time, Casey and Nathan could hear the distant echoes of laughter and the clinking of glasses even before they reached the entrance. With every step, Casey's heart raced faster.

Her synesthetic senses were on high alert.

As they entered the opulent space, Casey's senses were immediately overwhelmed with the mingling scents of wine, perfume, and the sound of hushed conversations. It was a cacophony of colors and textures in her mind; the sharp tang of citrus from a woman's perfume painted streaks of yellow across her vision, while the deep notes of an aged red wine formed rich, velvety burgundy ribbons in the air.

"Focus," Nathan whispered, placing a gentle hand on her shoulder. "We'll find him."

Casey nodded, steadying herself with a deep breath. She drew upon old mentor, Dr. Evelyn Reed's teachings, using her synesthesia to hone in on the subtle details around her, searching for the elusive cologne that had sparked her suspicions earlier. The room was filled with people dressed in their finest attire, each one vying for attention as they admired the lavish artwork on display.

"Excuse me, would you like some champagne?" a waiter asked, extending a tray of delicate crystal flutes towards them.

"Thank you," Casey replied, accepting a glass. The bubbles tickled her nose, evoking a sense of effervescence that seemed to dance in the space between her thoughts. She took a small sip and scanned the room, trying to immerse herself in the atmosphere without losing sight of their objective.

"Keep your eyes on the big buyers," Nathan suggested, his voice low as he leaned in closer. "Someone like Darlo would want to make a statement."

Casey's gaze drifted from one affluent guest to another, each one more ostentatious than the last. Their laughter was like glittering jewels scattered across a dark canvas; the silky tones of their voices wove intricate patterns around her, making it difficult to discern anything of significance.

"Wait," she whispered, her eyes narrowing as she caught a hint of a familiar scent. It was almost drowned out by the overpowering aroma of expensive perfumes, but there was no mistaking it – the vibrant red cologne from earlier.

"Over there," Casey whispered to Nathan, her eyes locked on a man near the edge of the room. He wore a sleek black suit that seemed to absorb the ambient light and a blood-red tie that stood out like a fresh wound against his pale skin. The sight of him sent a shiver down her spine, as if she were running her fingers along the lush texture of velvet.

"Is that him?" Nathan asked, his voice strained with anticipation.

"Let's find out." She replied, her heart pounding in her chest as they moved closer to the man.

As they wove through the sea of elegantly dressed guests, Casey's senses were assaulted by a cacophony of colors, scents, and sensations. Despite the overwhelming stimuli, she kept her focus on their target, knowing that one false move could be the difference between success and failure.

"Excuse me," Casey muttered to a woman draped in emerald silk as they edged closer to the man in the black suit.

As they approached the man, he suddenly turned to look at them; for a moment, he looked disinterested, but then his eyes moved to the weapons on their hips, visible past their jackets; his eyes widened. For a moment, time seemed to slow to a crawl, as if the universe itself held its breath in anticipation.

Robert Darlo hissed through gritted teeth, the facade of calm composure slipping away to reveal a man on the brink of panic. Without a word, he turned on his heel and sprinted towards the back of the room, his desperate flight leaving a trail of destruction in his wake.

Priceless paintings tumbled from their easels, the delicate frames splintering as they collided with the marble floor. The sound of shattering glass filled the air, accompanied by the horrified gasps of the stunned attendees.

"Stop him!" Nathan shouted, his voice cutting through the chaos like a knife. Casey set off in pursuit.

She pushed through the panicked crowd, her synesthetic perceptions honing in on the trail left by Darlo's distinctive cologne.

Casey's pulse quickened as she and Nathan darted through the bewildered attendees, their faces a blur of shock and indignation. The vibrant colors that swirled around her intensified with each pounding step.

"Watch out!" Nathan warned, grabbing Casey's arm just as an expensive-looking sculpture teetered precariously on its pedestal, threatening to topple onto them. Together, they sidestepped the potential disaster, their movements synchronized in perfect harmony.

"Thanks," she breathed, sparing him a grateful glance before returning her focus to the chase.

But the brief distraction had given Darlo a headstart. Her instincts screamed at her to keep moving, to follow the trail of vibrant red that seemed to bleed through the air as if painted by an invisible brush. It was a twisted breadcrumb trail that led them ever deeper into the heart of the art auction, where chaos reigned supreme.

"Darlo went this way," Casey whispered to Nathan as they rounded a corner, her voice barely audible above the din of panicked voices and shattering glass. She could feel the sensation of velvet caressing her senses, whispering to her that they were close – so tantalizingly close.

The frantic rhythm of their pursuit guided them toward a large display room at the back of the auction. The door slammed shut with a resounding bang, echoing like a gunshot through the already tense atmosphere. Casey and Nathan exchanged a look, their expressions a mix of determination and apprehension.

"Stay sharp," Nathan murmured, his hand instinctively hovering near his sidearm as they cautiously approached the entrance to the room. "He could be armed."

"Agreed," Casey replied, her mind racing with the possibilities.

As they eased open the door and stepped into the dimly lit room, Casey's breath caught in her throat.

CHAPTER THIRTEEN

The space was a labyrinth of towering racks and shadowy alcoves, each one filled with masterpieces that seemed to stare down at them with silent judgment. The room was filled with priceless works of art, each one more breathtaking than the last. Paintings adorned the walls, while sculptures of marble and bronze stood sentinel in the corners. It was a veritable treasure trove, a collection that would be coveted by any art enthusiast in the world.

"Mr. Darlo!" Nathan called out, his voice strong and unwavering. "There's nowhere left for you to run. Give yourself up peacefully, and we can end this without any more damage."

The room remained ominously silent, save for the distant echoes of the commotion outside. Casey scanned the area, her senses straining to detect any hint of their quarry. But the overwhelming cacophony of colors and textures threatened to drown out any hope of pinpointing his location.

"Keep looking," she thought, steeling herself against the sensory onslaught. "He's here somewhere."

Casey closed her eyes, allowing herself to focus solely on the synesthetic gift that had led her this far.

"Wait," Casey murmured, her concentration unwavering. The faintest sensation of velvet brushed against the edges of her consciousness, and she honed in on it with laser-like precision. "There. I think I've got something."

"Where?" Nathan asked, his hand instinctively reaching for his gun once more.

"Over there." Casey pointed towards a wall covered in abstract paintings, their vibrant hues blending together in a dizzying display of artistic expression. The scent of oil paint and varnish filled the air, mingling with the residual traces of cologne that still clung to her senses.

Nathan moved closer to the wall, his experienced eyes scanning the artwork for anything out of the ordinary. But it was Casey's heightened perception that guided her hand towards one particular canvas, its swirling pattern of reds and blues concealing the telltale outline of a hidden door.

"Here," she announced softly, pressing her palm against the cool surface. To her surprise, the door swung open without resistance, revealing a narrow passage that led deeper into the building.

"Nice work," Nathan muttered. "Darlo knows this place."

"Casing the joint?" she guessed.

"Who the hell is this guy?"

As they stepped through the hidden doorway.

They crept through the dimly lit passage, their footsteps muffled by the thick carpet underfoot. Casey's heart pounded in her chest, its frenetic rhythm amplified by the stillness that enveloped them. Nathan's hand rested on her shoulder, a steady presence that grounded her amidst the swirling vortex of sensations that threatened to overwhelm her.

As they reached the end of the corridor, they found themselves in a small room filled with an eclectic array of art and antiques. Robert Darlo stood at the far end, desperately trying to pry open a window that didn't seem to want to budge.

"Robert Darlo," Nathan announced, his voice measured and firm. "You're under arrest."

The man spun around to face them, his eyes wide with shock as he took in their determined expressions. For a moment, time seemed to stand still as the three of them regarded one another, each acutely aware of the delicate balance that held their fates in its grasp.

"Come peacefully, and no one gets hurt," Casey added, her gloves tightening imperceptibly around her weapon.

"Fine," he said after a tense pause, raising his hands in surrender. "You've got me."

"Keep your hands where we can see them," Nathan instructed, deftly securing Robert's wrists with handcuffs. He kept his gaze trained on the suspect, seasoned instincts ensuring that he remained alert for any sign of resistance.

As they led Robert out of the room, Casey couldn't help but wonder who he was, and why he'd given himself up so quickly after seeming intent on escape.

"Lawyer," Darlo muttered.

"Sure. But you're coming with us," Nathan retorted, his voice a growl, his eyes narrowed.

Casey fell into step behind them, looking towards the painting on the wall, then back towards the man they'd apprehended.

He seemed calm now. Relaxed.

She hesitated.

"Wait," she murmured.

"What?" Nathan said quickly.

She paused, staring at the man.

He had a *passable* resemblance to the man she'd glimpsed earlier. But the textures were all wrong.

She paused now, turning. She examined the man in custody.

His suit was wrinkled. "Your pants are on backwards," she said softly, pointing.

Nathan glanced down at Darlo's pants.

Indeed, the button was on the back, along with the zipper.

He shrugged. "New style."

Casey paused. "Cash? Did he offer you cash?"

"Who?" the man asked.

"Robert Darlo!" she demanded. "Where is he? Robert?" she called, glancing around the room. "I know you're in here.

Only quiet met her calls.

Now, Nathan looked confused, but Casey was nodding to herself. The man they were chasing, the one who'd changed his name, conned his way into an art auction, then sweet-talked this man into changing clothes with him--or perhaps this man was in on an escape plan all along--he was clearly a con artist. A grifter by trade.

Was he also their murderer?

She looked around the room. Then, I spotted the large, red sofa in one corner.

She approached it slowly, eyes narrowed.

As she drew near, she heard the faint, labored puffs of heavy breathing.

With a quick wave of her hand, Nathan understood the silent command and positioned himself at the opposite end of the sofa. Together, they lifted it with ease, revealing the real Robert Darlo laying prone on the ground, his chest heaving with exertion as he fought to catch his breath.

"Robert," she called out softly. "It's over."

He stared up at her, dust swirling around his face, and sneezed once.

He glared at her.

She didn't glare back, but just watched him closely.

He was shorter than the other man, chubbier, too. He had a bit of a waddle to his walk, like a penguin, as he stood up.

67

And his gut extended over his suit. He'd been sucking it in before, but now, he was too beleaguered to inhale deeply.

"Lawyer!" he said.

"The two of you, both," said Casey.

"He made me do it!" said the man in the backward pants. "Offered me a grand. Said it was to prank his friends!"

"Liar!" Robert said. "He's in on it. He's the one who put *me* up to it!"

"Bullshit, I am! Asshole!"

The two men started bickering, yelling back and forth at each other as Nathan procured a second pair of handcuffs.

"That's enough," he said, firmly. "You're both under arrest."

And with that, he cuffed Robert alongside the other man.

Casey and Nathan escorted the two men, who were still bickering, towards the exit.

"Henry, you bitch," said the one who'd pretended to be Robert. "You said this was an easy gig."

"Shut up, John," snapped Robert Darlo, a.k.a Henry. "They don't have shit. They don't have *anything*!" he yelled, turning to glare at Nathan.

"No. Just you on a murder charge," Nathan said conversationally.

The moment he said it and pushed the two men back out into the main hall, Henry and John both gaped.

"W-what?" said John, the associate.

"Hang on, now," Henry, the con artist, exclaimed. "Murder? What the hell? What murder?"

"Nice try," Nathan retorted. "Now move."

"No... no, hang on one moment," John protested. "He didn't say anything about no murder. He said it was just a little painting."

"Shut up, John!"

"No, screw you, man. I'm not taking a murder rap for you. No-- dammit. He's the mastermind. He paid me to help. We were going to steal a painting, that's it. Borrow really!" he rattled this all off so fast that Nathan didn't have a chance to get a word in edgewise.

"Fine," Nathan said eventually, the corners of his mouth twitching as if he found the whole thing quite amusing. "You two can sort this out back at the station, huh? Nice and loud, with us present."

The bickering continued as the men were shoved down the marble steps, and past a large number of audience members who watched while wearing expressions of supreme disapproval.

"Hey! Hey, wait a minute!" a security guard called out.

Casey flashed her badge.

And he stopped. "Who's going to pay for the damage?" the guard called.

"You'll get a call!" Nathan retorted.

And then they were shoving their two suspects--still bickering--into the car.

Casey felt her stomach turn, and she wondered if they were closer to solving the case... or if they'd just started pulling on a piece of yarn that had yet to completely unravel.

CHAPTER FOURTEEN

The sound of heavy footsteps echoed through the narrow corridor as Casey and Nathan approached the interrogation room. The sterile scent of antiseptic filled the air, and fluorescent lights flickered overhead, giving the scene an eerie quality. Casey's gloved fingers tightened around the file she carried, while Nathan adjusted the weight of his holstered gun against his hip.

As they entered the room, the atmosphere thickened. A single, dimly lit tube bulb extended from the ceiling, casting stark shadows across the cold, gray walls. In the far corner, a pudgy figure sat slumped on a metal chair bolted to the floor. Robert Darlo's arms were crossed defiantly, and he stared at them with an icy glare that would have made lesser investigators falter.

"Robert Darlo," Casey began, her voice steady and measured, as she placed the file on the table between them.

John Harlow, Darlo's associate, sat next to him, his body language mirroring that of Darlo—arms crossed, jaw clenched, eyes cold and unyielding. Like two sides of a tarnished coin, they presented an impenetrable wall of defiance. But they were also seated well apart, as the two of them had been bickering on the ride over but stoically silent since entering the station.

Harlow's thin, lanky frame shifted uncomfortably as the two agents acknowledged them.

"Mr. Harlow," Casey began, her voice steady despite the storm of color she perceived around the suspects. "We'd like to ask you a few questions as well."

"Go ahead," he replied tersely, his words clipped and flat. "But it's like I told you. None of this was my idea."

Casey couldn't help but notice how the shades of anxiety and deception swirled around both men like tendrils of smoke. It was a dance of shadows and light, where every step seemed choreographed to conceal something sinister just beneath the surface. As she locked eyes with John, she felt the colors shift and undulate, their patterns elusive and ever-changing.

"Can you tell us where you were on the night of October 21st?" she asked, her gaze never leaving his.

"Same place as him," John said, jerking his head toward Darlo. "At a bar. You got a problem with that?"

"No," Nathan interjected, his tone casual but firm. "We're just trying to get a clear picture of what happened that night."

"Look," John spat out, his frustration mounting. "I already told the other cops everything I know. I don't know nothing about no murder."

"Mr. Harlow," Casey said, "we're not accusing you of anything just yet. We just need to understand what happened."

She tapped her fingers against her arm, studying him. For now, she was waiting.

She shot a quick look to Nathan, exchanging a glance.

He glanced nearly imperceptibly back at the door.

The two of them were waiting for results on the fingerprint analysis of Robert Darlo.

They'd found another ID with the name Connor Flannery. They'd also discovered his alias for the craft show.

In the end, it boiled down to a simple question: who the hell did they have in their interrogation room?

And that's why they were stalling...

Waiting for the fingerprint results to come back.

For now, they'd decided to approach the suspects cautiously, without cracking any skulls just yet.

Casey's eyes narrowed, her focus unwavering as she studied the two recalcitrant suspects. Her synesthesia painted the air with vibrant colors of anxiety and deception, each hue a complex dance of truth and lies. At her side, Nathan remained cool and collected, his street-smart instincts matched with an uncanny ability to read people.

And he was watching the two of them like a hawk.

A sudden knock on the door startled them all, causing Casey's heart to skip a beat. As the door opened, a tech stepped into the room, clutching a manila folder in his hands. He looked nervous, glancing around at the tense occupants of the room before clearing his throat.

"Agent Hayes, Agent Bolt," he said, addressing them both. "We've got the results."

"Thank you," Nathan replied, reaching out to accept the folder. As he opened it, Casey noticed the tattoos on his knuckles tapping against the folder.

Nathan scanned the contents.

"Interesting," Nathan murmured under his breath, breaking Casey from her reverie. She turned her attention to him, curiosity piqued by the hint of surprise in his voice.

Darlo was staring at him, shifting uncomfortably in his chair.

"What is it?" Casey said.

But Nathan addressed their suspect.

"Robert Darlo, or should I say, Mr. Multiple Aliases," he began, handing over a stack of printouts to Casey. "We've discovered that our friend here has quite an extensive criminal history that spans across five states."

Casey's heart hammered in her chest as she rifled through the documents, the colors of deception and anxiety swirling around Darlo in her synesthetic vision. She could see the reds and yellows bleeding into one another, creating an intricate dance that seemed both chaotic and calculated. This man was more than just a suspect; he was a master manipulator who had evaded capture for years.

"Tanner Vosloo," she read. "Stefan Jeeter. Aaron Karl..." She whistled. "List just keeps going, huh? Larceny. Grand larceny. Theft. Burglary. You're a con artist, then... By trade."

"Damn," Nathan muttered under his breath, peering over Casey's shoulder at the seemingly endless list of crimes attributed to their uncooperative guest. "This guy's been busy."

Darlo was a conman, a grifter who had been running scams and swindling people for years. And now, they had him cornered.

"Robert Darlo," Casey began, her voice steady and confident as she met his defiant gaze, "or should I call you by one of your many other names?"

Darlo's jaw tightened, but he remained silent, his eyes never leaving Casey's face.

"Mr. Darlo," Casey continued, her analytical mind working overtime as she pieced together the puzzle before her. "Where were you on the nights of the 15th, 16th, and 17th?"

As she asked the question, Casey's heartbeat quickened in anticipation, her eyes locked onto Darlo's face. Nathan leaned back against a wall, the gray hue of his eyes reflecting the dim glow of the overhead lights. His tattoos seemed to fade into the shadows, the word "Bless" barely visible on his knuckles. He watched the exchange closely.

"Those nights... I was with my girlfriend at our apartment," Darlo responded hesitantly, his defiance from earlier fading away. "We were watching movies, ordering takeout... regular stuff."

72

"Can anyone verify your alibi?" Casey pressed.

"Yeah. She can. So can the neighbors. Nosy bastards have a ring camera on their door."

Casey hesitated.

The alibi had come seamlessly. He hadn't even hesitated.

"Like I said!" Robert insisted. "I ain't no murderer."

"We know about your fake name at the craft fair."

John looked at Robert, raising an eyebrow. "What craft fair?"

"So sue me," snapped Robert. "I had some business on the side."

Nathan interjected. "Suing is civil. We throw people in prison."

Robert didn't seem to find the joke too funny.

"We want to know about the altercation you had at the craft show."

"What altercation?" He sniffed.

"Sir. We've already spoken to two separate witnesses."

He sighed, rubbing at his jaw and adjusting his shirt where a roll of his belly had lodged against the fabric. "I mean... *shit,*" he said. "I just had a word is all."

"With another man's wife?"

"I like women. It's a weakness." He grinned in Casey's direction in a way that made her distinctly uncomfortable.

She leaned forward, "Do you know anything about a murder at a winery?"

He stared at her.

She just stared back. She consciously didn't provide the victim's name, hoping that he might volunteer a piece of information that only the killer might know.

But he stared blankly at her.

John, on the other hand, who'd remained mostly quiet up to this point, just shook his head, muttering under his breath.

"I didn't kill anyone," Robert said slowly. "And I sure as hell don't know about any winery."

"What about drowning in a bathtub?"

"What the hell?" he said, his face turning red. "No! Hell no! I don't... I don't do that." He pointed a finger adamantly at the file in Nathan's hand. "Look. See? I do have a rap sheet. Fair. but Do I kill? Hmm? Non violent. none of those were violent!"

"Burglary," Nathan pointed out.

"Threat. Not actual. Just a *threat.*"

Nathan hesitated, glancing at Casey.

She was frowning at the rap sheet now. He had a point. And he had an alibi.

She hesitated, then pushed to her feet. "We're going to need a name for your girlfriend. And that neighbor of yours with the camera."

"Like I told you," he began.

"We're not going to take your word for it," Casey interjected.

"Fine, fine... here, I"ll do you one better. Her number is in my phone. So is theirs. I'm telling you, I didn't have anything to do with it."

"We'll see," Casey said, and her stomach twisted in anxiety.

CHAPTER FIFTEEN

The soft purr of the engine seemed to amplify Casey's sinking feeling as she navigated her way back to the motel, the weight of defeat pressing down on her.

The alibis had checked out.

But part of her had known they would.

And now, they were back at square one. Her eyes darted between the road and the rearview mirror, observing her own reflection – dark hair pulled back in a tight ponytail to avoid the distracting sensation of it brushing against her skin. She flexed her fingers within her gloves, trying to contain the colors that threatened to spill over from her synesthetic mind.

"Damn it," she muttered under her breath, her frustration evident in the tightness of her jaw. She gripped the steering wheel harder.

Nathan sat next to her, but kept quiet, his eyes on the road ahead.

As she pulled into the motel parking lot, the sky above was a canvas of deep black intertwined with streaks of light from bright moon. With a heavy sigh, she killed the engine and stepped out of the car, the cool evening air caressing her face.

She looked around the desolate area, feeling the solitude wrapping around her like a shroud.

"Long day?" Nathan Hayes asked, his rugged features and salt-and-pepper hair caught the moonlight, giving him an almost ethereal glow.

"Exhausting," she admitted, her voice barely audible. "We're back to square one."

"Hey, don't worry about it. We'll find something eventually," he said, offering her a reassuring smile. Although his words were meant to comfort her, she could see the fatigue etched on his face, betraying his own doubts.

"Thanks, Nathan. I appreciate it." She offered a weak smile in return, then turned toward the entrance of the motel.

A cheap, street-facing room. Nathan's was next to hers.

"Hey, Casey."

She glanced back at the agent. He watched her, a slight frown creasing his features. He leaned with one hand against the metal rail circling the ground-floor motel rooms.

He hesitated, studying her. Then just gave a small, sad shake of his head. "It'll work out."

She nodded in his direction. "I hope so," she murmured.

For a moment, it almost looked like the handsome, rugged agent wanted to say more.

She didn't mind watching Nathan Hayes--in fact, it was one of the perks of their partnership. Of course, things had never gone beyond viewing pleasure. The HR office was quite adamant about workplace relationships. Besides, Casey had enough on her plate as it was.

The thought troubled her, and her mind briefly flitted to her own upbringing. To the constant *drain* of not knowing... her mother's case... her father's distance.

She grimaced, shaking her head as if to dislodge the thought.

Now, she felt as if her own exhaustion was bleeding out and seeping into every crack of the sidewalk.

She gave him a quick, weary smile then turned.

The door to her room creaked as she pushed it open, the dim lighting casting long shadows on the walls. She stepped inside, the atmosphere of solitude clinging to her like a second skin. The faint scent of stale cigarettes and cheap air freshener assaulted her senses – an unwelcome intrusion into her already turbulent thoughts.

Casey closed the door behind her, shutting out the world and all its disappointments for the night. She leaned against the door, taking a deep breath to center herself, her gloved hands pressing against the cool surface. In the darkness of the room, the colors of her synesthesia seemed even more vivid, a chaotic whirlwind of sensation that she struggled to keep at bay.

"Tomorrow," she whispered, steeling herself for another day in a long line of days spent chasing ghosts.

She removed her gloves, the colors seeping through her fingers like watercolors bleeding onto a white canvas, and allowed herself a moment to embrace the chaos within.

Then, her phone buzzed from within her pocket, jolting her back to reality. The vibration sent a shiver down her spine. She pulled the device out and glanced at the screen, her brows knitting in confusion as she read the name displayed: "Zach."

"Hey, stranger," the message read. "Long time no talk. How've you been?"

She stared at the name, surprised.

Partly, surprised she still even had his number saved in her phone. Casey hesitated, her finger hovering over the screen. It had been years since she'd spoken with Zach, an old college sweetheart who had once made her heart race with anticipation. But those days were long gone, buried beneath the rubble of the passage of time.

She frowned, equal parts surprised and confused. She could feel the pull of the past, the sweet temptation of nostalgia tugging her backward. But she knew that road only led to pain and disappointment, so she forced herself to focus on the present – on the work that needed her attention.

Another message. *I saw you on the news. Wow! You're a fed now?*

She just stared at the message, fingers hovering.

It had been some time since she'd been with a man or in any serious relationship.

She'd only had one fling since Zach, in fact.

But now...

Why was he reaching out?

She sighed, lowered the phone and didn't reply.

The dim light from the motel room's lone lamp cast eerie shadows on the walls, their distorted shapes dancing in sync with Casey's thoughts.

But as she lay down on the stiff motel mattress, the weight of unanswered questions refused to retreat. Images danced through her thoughts – crime scene photos, witness statements, her mother's cold, lifeless eyes staring at her from the past.

Her mother.

She frowned, eyes closed, laying in bed.

Not *this* case.

Another case.

Fifteen years ago.

Her mother...

The thoughts were swirling now.

The night was the worst. She wasn't able to distract herself at night. At night, the thoughts came rushing in, fast and inundating her senses.

Casey's mind drifted back to the case that had haunted her for years. The case that had driven her to become an FBI agent in the first place. The case that had taken her mother away from her.

It hadn't just taken her mother, though, had it?

She felt another pang of pain.

Her father... He'd never been the same. They had barely spoken in years now. No real meaningful connection existed between them.

This thought alone caused her heart to ache, and she felt a jolt of pain lance through her chest.

Pain, given her gift, had all sorts of unique reactions that could be felt in her body. Once, when stepping on a nail, she'd felt the flavor of grape gum in her mouth.

And whenever she thought of her mother, or her estranged father, her chest would ache and heart would palpitate.

She sat up abruptly, her chest heaving with emotion. She couldn't let herself fall down that rabbit hole again. She had to focus on the case at hand.

But the memories were relentless. They clawed at her mind, refusing to be ignored. She got out of bed, her feet padding softly on the threadbare carpet. She needed to clear her head.

She walked out of the motel room, the night air chill against her bare arms. She walked aimlessly, her mind lost in a sea of memories. She didn't know how long she walked for, but eventually she found herself standing in front of the attached bar in the back of the street-level motel.

The neon sign flickered above her head, illuminating her face in a garish red light. She hesitated for a moment before pushing open the door and stepping inside.

The bar was empty save for a lone bartender, wiping down glasses behind the counter. He looked up as she entered, nodding in greeting.

"What can I get you?" he asked, his voice gruff.

Casey hesitated for a moment before ordering a whiskey, neat. She took the glass and sat down at the bar, the liquid burning its way down her throat as she swallowed.

She felt a presence next to her and turned to see Nathan emerging from a back door.

For a moment, he paused, staring at her.

He hesitated as if half wanting to retreat.

She said, "Caught me."

He smirked at her. "Couldn't sleep?"

She shook her head.

He sat down next to her, and raised a couple fingers. "Sprite," he said.

The bartender just nodded, bringing Nathan his non-alcoholic drink.

She glanced at him. "Not a partaker?"

"Not anymore," he said.

"Oh. Sorry." She pushed her own drink away, as if hoping by pushing it out of view it might not offend him.

"Don't worry about it," he said, rubbing a hand through his disheveled hair.

The two of them sat hunched, equally tired, and equally lost in their own thoughts.

"Case got you up?" Nathan asked.

"Yeah," she said. But she didn't mention *which* case. "You?"

He shrugged. "Not really."

He took a drink of his Sprite, ice cubes swirling in the bubbly drink, clinking against the glass.

Casey closed her eyes, and found that sitting next to Nathan, she felt oddly comforted.

His presence had always been a source of... protection. He had her back, and such a thing couldn't be under-appreciated.

The exhaustion that had been building throughout the day began to overtake her, but was held at bay by the cacophony of colors and textures that swirled in her mind. Her synesthesia painted each memory with vivid hues, transforming them into a kaleidoscope of sensory experiences. In that chaos, she could almost hear her mother's voice echoing softly across the years.

"Casey, my sweet girl," the tender words seemed to whisper, momentarily soothing her troubled thoughts. "Never forget that you are strong, brave, and capable of anything."

As the memories continued to swirl, Casey found herself drowning in a sea of colors, the lines between reality and memory blurring together. She struggled to stay afloat, her thoughts racing through the fragments of the past, searching for something solid to cling to. But the more she tried to hold on, the more those fleeting images slipped away like sand through her gloved fingers.

She took a sip of her whiskey, allowing the burning drink to numb her senses. Nathan glanced at her, concern etched on his face.

"You okay?" he asked, his voice soft.

She took a deep breath, trying to steady herself. "Just tired," she replied, her voice barely above a whisper.

Nathan nodded, understanding in his eyes. "I get it," he said. "The job can do that to you."

She nodded, grateful for the understanding. They sat in silence for a while longer, the only sound the tinkling of ice in Nathan's glass.

Finally, Casey pushed away from the bar. "I should go back," she said, gesturing towards the motel room.

Nathan nodded. "Yeah, me too."

They walked out of the bar together, the neon sign flickering above their heads as they stepped out into the cold night air. They paused for a moment, the silence heavy between them.

"Nate," Casey said, breaking the silence. "Thanks for... You know. Helping on the case."

Nathan shrugged, a small smile tugging at the corners of his lips. "I'm paid too."

She just shrugged, but he smiled, nodding, as if sharing a quiet understanding.

She nodded, turning to leave. But before she could take a step, Nathan's hand was on her arm, stopping her.

"Casey," he said, his voice low. "I...I know this isn't the time or place, but...there's something I need to tell you."

Casey turned to face him, her heart racing in her chest. "What is it?" she asked, her voice barely above a whisper.

For a moment, she thought of the text message from Zach. She stared at Nathan, meeting those dark, piercing eyes. His jawline looked even sharper somehow, along with that intentional stubble.

He swallowed. "I... I lost someone. Not long ago," he said. "Came to the feds for a fresh start."

She blinked. This wasn't what she'd been expecting. She'd known him for long enough that she felt a bit hurt that he hadn't revealed this to her before... But Nathan was a guarded sort, and she'd known at least this. She allowed him to continue without interrupting.

His hand fell. "This case... reminds me of her."

Casey felt a jolt of compassion. "I'm sorry," she said softly.

"Just... You know, sometimes. I know I can get intense." He shrugged apologetically. "Anyway, not trying to be an emotional asshole."

He looked embarrassed all of a sudden, his features red.

His hand, which had been gently resting on her arm, withdrew suddenly, as if he were afraid it might get burned. He patted her jovially on the shoulder. Maybe even a bit harder than was necessary. "Good night, Cas. Just thought you should know."

He turned and sauntered away, chest puffed, arms swinging at his side, muscles visible.

He didn't look back.

She watched him leave, then released a long, pent-up sigh.

She turned back to the motel door.

And a quiet voice called from her memories.

"Find me, Casey," the ghostly echo implored, beckoning her to delve deeper into the darkness.

She just shook her head, sighing. She ignored the text. Ignored Nathan as well.

And she ignored the echoing voice gnawing at her subconscious.

Tomorrow, bright and early, she had to find this killer. It would make everything sane again.

CHAPTER SIXTEEN

The morning sun seeped through the curtains, casting a soft glow on Casey's face as she stirred beneath the cool sheets. Her dreams had been troubling, threatening to rouse her every few moments. Her body felt heavy, weighed down by the dark tendrils of sleep that clung to her consciousness. But there was no time for rest; the case demanded her attention, and she willed herself awake.

With reluctance, Casey pushed back the covers, put her gloves back on from where they rested on the night-stand, and swung her legs over the bed while adjusting the covers, her gloved hands making little sound against the smooth fabric. She sat there for a moment, gathering her thoughts, the loose strands of her dark hair brushing against her cheeks in a dance that would have driven her mad if she allowed the fringe to go wild throughout the day. The room was still as if holding its breath.

Suddenly, the silence shattered as her phone screamed to life, demanding her attention like a petulant child. The shrill ring sent a jolt of adrenaline racing through her veins. Her heart thundered in her chest, an anxious drumbeat echoing through her mind as she grabbed the device.

"Bolt," she answered, her voice tense with anticipation.

"Casey, we've found another one," Nathan's voice was grave, the words falling like stones in the pit of her stomach. "Body drowned in a vat at a vineyard."

She just sat there, staring.

"Casey?"

"We're sure it's the same guy?"

"Same MO."

"We're sure..." she trailed off. Of course, they were sure. She shook off the last vestiges of denial, frowning and steeling herself.

"Four... That makes it four..." she whispered, the numbers swirling in her head like crimson clouds. Her synesthetic senses painted the scene in vivid hues of terror, each victim's last moments etched in shades of scarlet and violet. Casey could feel the threads of the case intertwining, beckoning her further into the twisted labyrinth of the killer's design.

"Where?" she asked, her tone firm, masking the unease gnawing at the edges of her thoughts.

"Stonewoods Vineyards," Nathan replied. "I'm headed there now. Meet me as soon as you can."

"Understood. On my way."

***

The sun was just beginning to rise over the horizon as Casey and Nathan pulled up to Stonewoods Vineyards, casting a warm glow on the vast expanse of grapevines that stretched out before them. Rows upon rows of leafy greens and rich purples seemed to go on forever, creating a sense of eerie isolation.

"Quite a place for a murder," Nathan remarked, breaking the silence that had hung between them since they left the city behind. His voice was low, almost somber, reflecting the gravity of the situation.

"Let's hope we can find something for once," Casey replied, her voice equally subdued. She could feel the weight of the case pressing down on her, threatening to crush her like the grapes that surrounded them.

A large door was propped open by two saw-horses bedecked in caution tape.

A few police officers were standing there. An ambulance could be seen pulling in from the distance, while a coroner's van was navigating around it, amidst a cloud of dust.

Another police officer was approaching them, the woman's hand waving in front of her face to clear the swirling dust kicked up by the tires.

The woman raised a hand.

"What happened?" Nathan said, without introducing himself, and skipping any formality.

"The body was found a few hours ago. Coroner has it now," said the cop.

"Who found it?" Nathan asked.

"The owner of the vineyard. Said one of the vats was leaking."

The cop gave a quick, uncomfortable shrug, stepping aside and gesturing towards the open doors leading into the storage space.

"Was the owner her early?"

"Yeah. He's not here--going to give his report at the station."

"Not here?" Nathan said.

She shrugged. "Knows the captain. Got a special accomodation."

Nathan shook his head in frustration.

Casey stepped forward, her gloved hand reaching out to touch Nathan's arm in a gesture of solidarity. "Let's focus on the case, Nathan," she said softly, her voice a soothing balm against the tension that crackled in the air. "We're here to find the killer, not worry about the politics."

Nathan nodded, his jaw clenching as he took a deep breath. "

Together, they stepped through the open doors and into the storage facility, their eyes scanning the area for any clues that might lead them to the killer. The air was thick with the scent of fermenting grapes, creating a heady atmosphere that made Casey's head spin. She focused on her breathing, willing herself to remain calm and focused. The scent of grapes mingled with the faint metallic tang of machinery. The vineyard was already coming to life, the distant sounds of workers and machines adding an unsettling hum to the otherwise tranquil scene.

A cop gestured, muttering something, and Nathan nodded.

He paused in front of the large vat in the back of the room.

"Here it is," Nathan said, gesturing to the vat where the latest victim had been discovered. The sight of the looming steel container sent a chill down Casey's spine – it was a morbid reminder of the horrors that had transpired.

Casey hesitated for a moment before stepping forward, her gloved fingers grazing the cold metal surface of the vat. Her synesthetic abilities immediately kicked into high gear, the texture of the metal setting off a web of colors and sensations in her mind. It felt like she was diving into a whirlpool of deep blues and silvers, each ripple sending a new wave of information coursing through her.

"Anything?" Nathan asked, his voice pulling her back to reality.

"Nothing yet," she muttered, but her eyes remained fixed on the vat, the colors swirling and dancing in her mind. She knew that somewhere within this chaotic symphony of sensations, there had to be a clue – something that would help her unravel the twisted threads of this case.

The body had already been moved once more.

But again, as with the last scene, she could see the puddle of wine on the ground where it had lain after being discovered.

Casey crouched down, her gloved hand hovering just above the damp stain on the concrete floor. She closed her eyes, focusing on the colors and textures that flooded her mind. The wine was a rich burgundy, almost black, in the dim light of the warehouse. The liquid was thick and sticky, with a metallic tang that set her teeth on edge.

Suddenly, a new sensation flooded her senses – a sharp, acrid smell that made her eyes water. She opened her eyes, looking around the room for the source of the scent. It was then that she noticed a small, inconspicuous door in the far corner of the warehouse. The door was made of heavy metal, with a small window set into the top. The glass was fogged over, making it impossible to see inside.

Without a word, Casey made her way across the room, her heart pounding in her chest. She felt like she was walking towards a trap, like a mouse lured in by the scent of cheese. But she couldn't ignore the pull of her instincts – something important was waiting for her behind that door.

She reached out, her gloved fingers grasping the cool metal of the handle. She took a deep breath, then pushed the door open.

The smell hit her like a brick wall – a noxious, overpowering stench that made her gag. She stepped back, her eyes watering as she took in the scene before her. The room was small, barely large enough to hold a single person. The walls and floor were covered in a film of grime and filth, and in the center of the room was a rotting pile of grapes.

She frowned, staring. And then her eyes moved to the window behind it.

The grapes had come from wooden crates.

And the stacks of crates had toppled due to the shattered window above.

"I think I found how he got in," she called over her shoulder.

She didn't look to see if Nathan was listening. She glanced along the jagged edges of the window, carefully. No sign of any fabric, or blood. Just shards of glass. Then, she clambered on top of one of the crates, avoiding any of the grapes, and slipped through the opening in the window.

It was a tight fit.

Did that mean the killer was thin?

Stepping outside the dimly lit storage room, Casey's senses were once again bombarded by the rich scents and sounds of the vineyard. The sun was rising higher in the sky now, casting elongated shadows across the rows of grapevines that stretched out before her. As she made her way around the building, she noticed something unusual. A frown creased her forehead as her eyes narrowed in on a set of tire treads imprinted in the damp earth.

"Hey, Nathan," Casey called out, gesturing for him to come over.

She heard the sound of footsteps as Nathan approached from the open doors of the storage space.

She was staring at the muddy tracks.

"Look at these treads. They seem familiar, don't they?"

"Maybe," Nathan replied, crouching down beside her to get a better look. "But there are probably hundreds of cars with similar tires."

"No, this is different. I remember seeing these exact ones somewhere else." Her brows furrowed as she tried to recall where she had seen them before. The frustration simmered beneath the surface, her synesthetic perception blaring colors as she concentrated, trying to make sense of the elusive memory.

"Alright, let me know if you figure it out. I'll check with the owner about any recent visitors," Nathan said, standing up and giving her shoulder a gentle squeeze before heading off.

Determined not to let the nagging feeling go unresolved, Casey pulled out her phone and began scrolling through the photos from previous crime scenes, hunting for a connection. She knew she couldn't simply rely on her memory – the onslaught of sensory information often made it difficult for her to separate one experience from another. But she was certain that if she could just find the right image, her synesthesia would help her recognize the link between sight and touch.

As she flicked through the images, an article caught her eye.

One of the earlier cases.

The woman who'd been drowned in a tub.

She remembered it now.

And as she stared at the photo, her eyes projected the same, itching sensation along her arms. The feeling she *now* felt while staring at the treads.

She blinked, hesitant. The image featured a photo of a jeep parked near the apartment of one of the earlier victims. The same distinctive tire treads were visible in the picture, and she felt a surge of triumph as her synesthetic senses confirmed the connection between the two sets of treads.

"Got it," she whispered to herself, her heart racing with excitement. "Nathan!" she called out, waving her phone in the air as she turned to find him. "I found it! The same treads, I'm sure of it!"

"Really?" Nathan hurried back over from where he'd been moving towards the office, his eyes wide with anticipation. "You think there's a connection?"

"Absolutely," Casey replied, her voice filled with conviction. "Look at this," Casey urged, thrusting her phone towards Nathan. The screen

86

showed the article she'd found, the jeep's tire treads unmistakable in the accompanying photo. "I knew I'd seen these treads before. They're identical to the ones here at the vineyard."

Nathan studied the image, his brow furrowing as he processed the implications. "Is... are you sure? Just looks like treads."

But she couldn't invite him into her mind. To *her,* it was obvious. Each tingle along her arm, the itch at her elbow--it would've sounded silly to anyone else. But it was unmistakable, the way her brain organized the patterns *just so.*

But before she could, or had to, defend herself, Nathan just nodded. "Of course, you're sure. This could be huge, Cas. If we can find out who owns that jeep, we might just have our killer."

She felt a flash of gratitude. He was consciously making it clear he wasn't questioning her. Casey nodded, her pulse quickening at the thought of finally making progress in the case.

"Let's get back to the station and run the license plate," Nathan suggested, already heading towards their car.

"Right behind you."

CHAPTER SEVENTEEN

A veil of mist hung in the air as Casey and Nathan's car wound its way up the serpentine mountain road, the dense evergreens on either side casting long shadows across their path. The atmosphere felt otherworldly, a fitting prelude to the mysterious country club that awaited them.

They'd found the jeep, and it had been surprisingly easy to trace it.

Casey's frown had something to do with this ease.

She stared through the window, peering up the road ahead.

"Here we are," Nathan muttered as they rounded the final bend, revealing an opulent estate nestled in a forest clearing. The sprawling stone and wood building radiated affluence, its grandiosity dwarfing the surrounding landscape.

As the car idled in the gravel parking lot, Nathan turned to face her. "So, tell me again, who owns the jeep?"

She glanced at him. "Our suspect is Charles Whitmore, wealthy businessman and exclusive member of this club.

"And the vehicle has no other owners?"

"None," she said. "His jeep was at two separate crime scenes."

"Good enough for me," Nathan replied, a determined glint in his eyes. "Let's see what we can find."

Casey nodded, pulling her gloves tighter around her fingers.

The country club's opulent stone and wood building loomed ahead, its warm lights flickering like a beacon in the gathering darkness.

"Look," Nathan whispered, pointing to a gleaming black jeep parked near the entrance. "There it is. He's still driving it."

Casey's heart skipped a beat at the sight, her synesthetic senses tingling with anticipation. She could see the colors emanating from the vehicle – deep blues and purples that spoke of power and wealth, with a touch of crimson that hinted at danger.

"Let's check it out," she suggested, her voice barely audible. They approached the jeep cautiously, their footsteps muffled by the gravel underfoot.

As they peered through the tinted windows, Casey's enhanced vision allowed her to pick up on the slightest details. She noticed a leather briefcase on the back seat, a pair of expensive sunglasses on the dashboard, and a faint scent of cologne lingering in the air. But despite her best efforts, there was nothing overtly incriminating to be found.

"Nothing here," she murmured, disappointment lacing her words.

"Seems that way," Nathan agreed, his eyes scanning the bumper and tires. "We need to get inside that country club and find our guy."

"Right," Casey replied, steeling herself for what lay ahead. As they made their way towards the imposing building, she couldn't help but feel a sense of foreboding. With each step, the atmosphere grew heavier; wealth in the wrong hands often had a suffocating effect.

The country club loomed before them like a fortress, its stone and wood facade imposing against the darkening sky. The scent of pine hung heavily in the air, mingling with the distant fragrance of cigars and expensive whiskey. Casey could feel her pulse quicken as they approached, the anticipation building within her like a coiled spring.

"Here we go," Nathan murmured, his voice low but steady. He adjusted his tie, the small gesture betraying his own nervousness despite his outward calm.

As they reached the entrance, their path was suddenly blocked by two imposing bouncers who crossed their massive arms over their chests, muscles bulging under tight black shirts. Their cold, calculating eyes seemed to bore into Casey and Nathan.

"May I help you?" one of the bouncers asked, his tone polite but firm.

"Good evening," Casey replied smoothly, attempting to charm them with her smile. "We were invited to join a friend for dinner this evening."

"Names?" the second bouncer demanded, his gaze never leaving theirs.

"Casey Bolt and Nathan Hayes," she answered confidently. They'd decided to avoid bringing up their credentials unless absolutely necessary.

Federal agents had a way of attracting all sorts of attention and causing mouths to seal shut.

So for now, Casey and Nathan wore their jackets over their holsters. Nathan was even keeping his knuckles, with the tattoo, hidden from sight, one hand bunched in his pocket.

The first bouncer checked a list on his clipboard, his brows furrowing as he scanned the names. "I'm sorry, but I don't see your names on the list," he said, looking back at Casey and Nathan. "I'm afraid you won't be able to enter tonight."

"Surely there must be some mistake," Casey tried again, her persuasive skills kicking into high gear. "Our friend is an exclusive member here, and he assured us that our names would be on the list."

"Like I said," the bouncer replied, his voice growing colder, "your names aren't on the list. Now, if you'll excuse us, we have other guests to attend to."

"Hang on," Nathan said, shooting her a glance.

Casey hesitated; she wanted to pry a bit more before going full federal, but clearly Nathan wasn't in the mood.

His badge appeared.

"We need to enter. Now."

The bouncers glanced at the badge. "You got that from a cereal box?" One of them snickered.

The other said, "Hopefully it comes with a warrant, otherwise there's shit-all I can do for you."

Nathan's eyes narrowed. "Don't need a warrant to enter a club."

"Private property," a man with short-cut hair replied. His eyes narrowed into mean slits. "Now bug off."

Casey sighed, not because she thought they'd been stymied in their efforts, but rather because she knew how Nathan could get when people start acting in such a way.

Her partner was now glaring. His hand with the tattoo had emerged from his pocket.

"Enough," Nathan muttered under his breath. He stepped forward, his boots crunching on the gravel pathway that led to the entrance.

One of the bouncers stepped in front of him, hand extended.

"Hey!" Nathan snapped, slapping the hand away. "You're obstructing an ongoing investigation. I suggest you let us through, or you'll be facing charges."

The bouncers exchanged smug glances, clearly unimpressed by Nathan's display of authority. One of them, a burly man with a shaved head and a thick neck, chuckled dismissively.

"Nice try," he sneered. "But this is private property. Your badge doesn't scare us."

"Besides," added the other bouncer, a tall, lean man with a sinister grin, "we've got some pretty powerful people on our side here. You think they're going to let a couple of cops waltz right in?"

As the bouncers laughed at their perceived invincibility, Nathan clenched his jaw, his anger barely contained.

"Private property or not," Nathan retorted, "obstructing justice is a crime. And I assure you, I have no problem putting you behind bars for it."

"Look, detective," the tall bouncer said, "I don't know who you think you are, but you're not getting past us. So why don't you and your little friend there just turn around and walk away?"

"Fine," Nathan said through gritted teeth, forcing himself to remain calm. "But remember, you two are making a choice here. A choice that could have serious consequences."

The bouncers merely smirked, their faces a portrait of arrogant defiance.

Nathan took a deep breath, and Casey muttered, "Keep it cool. Please. Keep it cool."

"Okay," Nathan said coolly, feigning surrender. "I guess we'll just have to come back with a warrant."

The taller bouncer's grin widened, clearly believing he had won. But Nathan was far from done. As the bouncer turned to gloat to his partner, Nathan acted swiftly, grabbing the man's wrist and twisting it behind his back. The element of surprise worked in his favor as he slapped the handcuffs on him.

"Obstruction of justice," Nathan growled into the bouncer's ear, pleased to see the shock register on the man's face. "You were warned."

Casey's eyes widened, her gloved hand covering her mouth as she watched the scene unfold.

With his partner restrained, the second bouncer's arrogance evaporated. Panic painted his features as he fumbled at his hip, fingers grasping for the gun holstered there. Nathan's instincts kicked in.

As the bouncer pulled out his weapon, Nathan launched himself forward, closing the distance between them in an instant. His hand shot out, expertly knocking the gun away before it could be aimed. The weapon clattered to the ground, spinning across the pavement like a child's toy.

Nathan didn't hesitate. He delivered a powerful blow to the bouncer's jaw. The man crumpled to the ground, unconscious.

As Nathan stood over the two incapacitated bouncers, he grimaced, glancing at Casey and said, "Sorry."

She sighed. "I thought you were going to keep it cool."

He looked down at the cuffed bouncer and the unconscious one. "This was me keeping it cool." He looked up, shrugged.

Casey just shook her head. She quickly checked the unconscious bouncer's pulse. Healthy and hearty, he'd be fine.

She felt a flicker of relief, but then refocused on the task at hand.

As Casey slipped past the bouncers, she stepped through the glass doors, and it was as if she were entering another world.

Her senses were suddenly bombarded by the opulent atmosphere of the exclusive gathering. The sound of champagne corks popping translated into bursts of vibrant color before her eyes. The mingling scents of expensive perfume and cologne created an intricate tapestry of hues and textures that she could almost reach out and touch.

"Casey, focus," Nathan's voice whispered in her earpiece, steadying her. "Remember what we're here for."

"Right," she murmured, reining in her synesthesia as much as possible to remain sharp and alert. She scanned the room, searching for any sign that might lead her to the owner of the jeep.

The crowd was an eclectic mix of people - businessmen and women clad in tailored suits, socialites draped in shimmering gowns, and others who seemed more at home in the shadows than under the chandeliers. Each interaction between the guests revealed fascinating connections that Casey's mind couldn't help but map out in a web of colors.

"Anything yet? Do you see Charles Whitmore?" Nathan asked, his hand pulling out his phone to check the DMV photo they'd been provided.

"Nothing," Casey replied, her dark hair pulled back tightly to avoid distracting her from the task at hand. She moved through the crowd with fluid grace, her gloved hands brushing against the sleeves of her long coat.

Time seemed to slow down as Casey's search intensified, the pressure mounting with each passing moment. She could feel her heart racing in her chest, beating like a metronome that counted down the seconds she had left before their suspect either slipped away or became aware of their presence. Her synesthesia, once a burden, now served as her compass, guiding her through the labyrinthine gathering with unwavering precision.

As she brushed past a woman draped in emerald silk, a scent caught her attention—rich leather and a hint of cedarwood. The combination resonated in her mind, manifesting as a deep shade of purple tinged with golden sparks.

She gave a quick smile to the woman, wondering if they'd met before.

Or perhaps it was the emotion of anxiety now swirling in her chest.

She watched the woman for a second, hesitant, but then shook her head.

No... No, sometimes, following instinct alone could be a distracting measure.

A sudden burst of laughter nearby drew her attention, and Casey found herself drawn toward a group of men clustered around a high-top table. One man, in particular, stood out—a tall figure with salt-and-pepper hair and a confident air that bordered on arrogance. He held a tumbler of amber liquid, the ice cubes clinking together as he gestured animatedly, his expensive watch glinting under the soft lighting.

He looked older than in the photo. She stared.

She studied the man from a safe distance. Her senses flared, the colors swirling around him like a kaleidoscope of damning evidence: the polished silver cufflinks, the faint wisps of tobacco smoke that clung to his clothes, and the timbre of his laughter that sent shivers down her spine. She had found him.

She began to turn to see if Nathan had spotted her.

But before she could, she noticed Mr. Whitmore move.

As if sensing her gaze, the suspect's eyes momentarily met hers. He hesitated, glancing at her as if sizing her up.

His brow furrowed, he hesitated, and then he turned and began walking away, moving quickly.

CHAPTER EIGHTEEN

Whitmore's expensive suit stood out as he moved hastily away from her. At the same moment, Casey's gaze landed on Nathan, who seemed to be veering off towards a cluster of security guards who'd noticed them.

Nathan gave her a quick nod as if to say *I've got this.*

"Damn," Casey muttered under her breath, wondering if she ought to back Nathan up or pursue their mysterious jeep owner.

She made a decision, locking her eyes on Whitmore's retreating figure.

As she trailed him through the opulent halls of the country club, Casey couldn't help but notice the increasing speed of Whitmore's stride. It was subtle at first, but soon enough, he was practically rushing away from her, forcing her to quicken her pace just to keep him in sight. Nathan would have to handle the security guards on his own.

"Mr. Whitmore!" she called out, her voice barely audible over the mingling crowd. If he heard her, he gave no indication, instead continuing his hurried escape.

"Whitmore, wait!" Casey tried again, louder this time, but he disappeared around a corner just as she rounded it herself.

She hoped he'd hit a dead end.

No such luck. He only seemed to move faster, darting through a set of double doors. Casey followed, her breaths coming in gasps now, her gloves slick with perspiration.

She burst into a kitchen, narrowly avoiding a collision with a waiter balancing a tray of champagne flutes. The staff hustled around her, their movements choreographed chaos as they prepped hors d'oeuvres and plated entrees. Heat from the ovens washed over her, and the scent of seared meat and simmering sauces filled her nostrils. She pushed through the bustle, the stark white tiles beneath her feet contrasting sharply with the vibrant red tomatoes being diced nearby.

"Excuse me!" she called out, sidestepping a sous chef carrying a large pot of steaming soup. Their faces were a whirlwind of colors in her mind, but she couldn't afford to pause and take it all in. Whitmore had already slipped out the back door, and she couldn't let him get away.

Out in the long hall, the darkness enveloped her like a heavy blanket, her footsteps echoing off the damp walls. She strained her ears, trying to discern any sign of Whitmore ahead. A faint shuffling sound caught her attention, and she hurried towards it, her hand instinctively resting on her gun.

As she rounded a corner, she was met with a short stretch of hall and a large double doors set with wooden inlays.

She hesitated. No other rooms in sight.

She paused briefly, glancing over her shoulder, then her hand moved to her gun, and she reached out pushing the door open.

An unsettling sight – a room filled with taxidermy animals and mounted antlers, their glassy eyes reflecting the dim light. The air was thick with a musty scent that sent shivers down her spine.

"Whitmore?" she called out tentatively, her voice quavering slightly as she stepped further into the room.

"Damn it," Casey muttered to herself, her pulse racing as she cautiously navigated through the eerie display.

The room's shadows seemed to stretch and coil, as if they were alive, and Casey felt the knot of anxiety in her chest tighten.

"Where are you?" she whispered, more to herself than anyone else. Her heart hammered against her ribcage, and she couldn't tell if it was fear or frustration that fueled the relentless pounding.

As Casey moved deeper into the shadowy space, she noticed how the taxidermy animals appeared almost lifelike in their frozen poses – a fox forever leaping at its prey, a deer caught mid-gallop. The unsettling details only served to heighten the tension that had taken root within her.

"Come on," she murmured, her gloved fingers tightening around the grip of her gun. She ducked behind a stuffed bear, its massive frame casting a foreboding shadow on the floor. The soft rustle of her footsteps mingled with the distant drip of a leaking pipe, creating an eerie soundtrack that set her nerves on edge.

She glanced behind a mounted elk head, its antlers splayed like skeletal fingers, but found nothing other than dust and shadows.

"Enough!" she snapped, her voice cracking with annoyance. "I'm done playing games, Whitmore. Show yourself!"

In the deafening silence that followed, Casey's breaths came in short, shallow gasps, her lungs struggling to draw in the stale air. Her mind raced with possibilities, each darker than the previous, as she continued her search through the unsettling menagerie.

As Casey's frustration mounted, her synesthesia flared to life, the colors of the room swirling together with the textures of the taxidermy animals. Her senses were assaulted by a cacophony of hues and sensations – the coarse fur of a bear blending with deep browns, the velvet antlers of a deer merging into soft greens, and the glassy eyes of various predators fusing with cold, unfeeling grays.

"Focus," she whispered to herself, trying to separate the sensory onslaught from her surroundings. "You need to find him."

The overwhelming mixture of colors and textures seemed to take on a life of their own, forming an ever-shifting labyrinth that threatened to swallow Casey whole. As much as she tried to ignore it, the synesthetic storm filled her mind, intensifying her unease and making it nearly impossible to concentrate.

In that moment, a sudden flash of movement caught Casey's attention. She turned toward a large window.

A figure stood silhouetted against the glass.

She jolted in surprise. Mr. Whitmore's figure watched her with a chilling intensity. The rifle in his hand gleamed ominously in the dim light, and as their gazes met, he raised the weapon and pointed it directly at her.

CHAPTER NINETEEN

The gun barrel pointed towards Casey like an accusing finger, and it was as if time seemed to slow.

Her senses were firing randomly, and she struggled to focus on any one thing.

The room was a cacophony of muted colors and lifeless eyes. A collection of taxidermy animals stood posed in various states of predatory readiness, their glassy stares seemingly fixated on her.

The low hum of an overhead light mingled with the shadows cast by the preserved creatures, lending an eerie atmosphere to the space.

She forced her misfiring senses to focus on the immediate threat.

Her heart skipped a beat at the sight of Whitmore's rifle barrel pointed directly at her chest. She could feel the coldness of the metal, even from several feet away; its dark gray hue clouded her vision like a storm brewing on the horizon. Despite the immediate danger, Casey maintained her calm demeanor, drawing on her years of experience in law enforcement. Her eyes locked onto Whitmore's, exuding confidence that belied the pounding of her heart.

"Easy now," she said softly, her voice steady despite the tension in the room. "No need for any sudden moves."

Whitmore's grip on the rifle tightened, beads of sweat forming on his brow as he weighed his options.

The man's expensive suit seemed like an encasing of armor now, and his expression wasn't nearly as smug as it had been back in the main room.

His silver hair was brushed aside by one flick of his hand, causing the rifle to wobble and dip before he caught it again and raised it once more.

In the stillness of the room, Casey watched the play of shadows across Whitmore's face, her mind racing to find a way to defuse the situation without risking either of their lives. She couldn't afford to let fear or panic cloud her judgment.

"Put the gun down, Whitmore," she commanded, her voice firm but gentle, as if she were trying to coax a frightened animal out of hiding.

The air in the room seemed to crackle with tension, as though charged by the dim, flickering light that cast the stuffed animals' shadows across the walls. The glassy eyes of a snarling wolf glinted in the half-light, while a stoic bear towered over them, its fur a mottled tapestry of grays and browns.

"Why the hell are you following me?" Whitmore snarled, finally seeming to find his voice.

"Whitmore," she began, her voice steady despite the rifle trained on her. "I'm Agent Casey Bolt with the FBI. Lower the gun."

As she spoke, her synesthetic perception painted the room in a mixture of sensations. The musty scent of the taxidermy mingled with the faint, metallic tang of fear, producing a swirling pattern of rust-red and burnt orange that danced at the edges of her vision. She felt the weight of Whitmore's gaze, a heavy, dark blue pressing down on her like a storm cloud, as if his uncertainty were manifesting itself in tangible form.

It was in moments like these that her gift *most* came to the forefront.

She could *sense* his uncertainty, despite his gruff tone. Could see it in the swirling colors; her senses picking up on something as small as a neck muscle twitch, or double-time breathing. It all coalesced into visual cues only she could discern.

Uncertainty could be an ally... it could also be a death knell if she didn't play her cards carefully.

"FBI?" Whitmore's voice wavered slightly, betraying his surprise. The barrel of the rifle dipped ever so slightly, reflecting a hesitant, pale yellow that shimmered and waned in Casey's mind. "How do I know you're telling the truth?"

Whitmore's reluctance was palpable, the air in the room heavy with an electric tension. His eyes flickered between Casey's face and the gun he held, the barrel wavering ever so slightly. It was as if he stood at the edge of a precipice, one false move away from plummeting into the abyss below.

With agonizing slowness, Casey produced her federal badge, holding it up so that the dim light caught the gleaming gold surface. She watched as Whitmore's eyes locked onto the badge, his expression shifting from suspicion to a grudging acceptance. The air in the room seemed to change, the oppressive weight of uncertainty giving way to the tentative beginnings of something else... fear?

"Okay," Whitmore said, lowering his rifle with visible reluctance. "You're legit. Now, why the hell are you following me?"

She blinked in surprise, staring at him.

He had lowered the gun.

If anything, some of his fear had diminished to be replaced by an air of confusion.

Was he acting?

If not... why had he lowered the gun? If he was the killer they'd suspected, wouldn't he have wanted to maintain his position of power?

She studied the man and the way his silver hair caught the moonlight in the window behind him. Sometimes, indirect was the way to go, but other times, playing cat paws games could only be distracting.

His uncertainty again stood out to her.

So she offered, in counter veiling point, a level of certainty in her comment. She didn't obfuscate, but said, directly, "I'm investigating a series of murders. Your jeep was spotted at several crime scenes," she began, her voice calm and steady.

He blinked, hesitated, and then his jaw unhinged slowly, lowering at the same speed as his rifle had. "W-what the hell? *Murder*?" he stared at her, stunned. "I... no!" he exclaimed. "I didn't have anything to..." he trailed off, gaping at her as if she'd slapped him.

Agian, she was taken by just how sincere his reaction seemed to be, but she knew better than most that looks could be deceiving.

Still, the uncertainty had churned and turned into an aura of astonishment.

She still wasn't picking up on any guilt.

Casey watched as Whitmore's expression shifted from astonishment to anger, his face contorting in a snarl. She could feel the sharp jolt of anger radiating off him, a bright red that crackled like flames in her mind.

It was as if she were watching his thoughts process in real time. A twitch of his cheek. A widening of his eyes, a dilation of the pupils, and it all translated to rage.

"Who the hell told you that? I haven't been to any goddamn crime scenes!" he spat, his eyes blazing with fury.

Casey held up a hand, her voice calm as she tried to soothe his anger. "We have surveillance footage of your jeep at the scenes, Mr. Whitmore."

She knew they were isolated, alone.

But this too was intentional. In an unsteralized environment like this, perhaps he'd be more willing to reveal something. This was familiar territory to him, so he had home turf advantage.

Her words seemed to hang in the air, heavy with accusation. Casey watched as Whitmore's expression shifted again, this time to one of disbelief. "No, that's not possible," he said, shaking his head. "I don't know what you're talking about."

Casey's senses were on high alert now, the kaleidoscope of colors swirling in her mind like a storm. She could sense the fear and uncertainty rolling off Whitmore, but there was something else, too...

"Your Jeep was seen at a vineyard this morning." This wasn't technically true, but the tire treads were a match. "And your jeep was also seen near a wine-tasting studio where a woman was drowned in her apartment."

The man stared at her, stunned.

She spoke matter-of-factly, without any accusation in her tone. She often found this allowed people more time to consider her words.

He frowned, then said, "I go to a lot of damn vineyards. Part of the job."

"And what's your job, sir?"

She faced him, all too aware of the gun in his hand trained on the ground, but her own hand resting on her holster now.

"I'm a wine distributor," Whitmore replied, his voice tight with frustration. "I travel a lot. I have nothing to do with those murders."

Casey studied him for a moment, weighing his words against her own intuition.

Again, no sign of guilt.

"I mean, hell--sometimes I even let my employees use my jeep," he said, shaking his head.

She frowned. "Where were you the last few mornings, Mr. Whitmore."

"Same place I always am," he retorted. "With my wife, at the pickle-ball court."

"Can she verify that?"

Whitmore was already pulling out a phone. He held up a finger in her direction as if to keep any further questions at bay.

He dialed a number, frowning as he did.

As he waited for his wife to pick up, Casey studied the shadows cast by the taxidermy animals on the walls, their eerie forms seeming to watch her every move.

She waited patiently, wondering if this was just another bluff.

But then a voice answered.

"Hey, honey," Whitmore said into the phone, his voice warm and affectionate. "Just had a quick question for you."

He made no mention of Casey. She watched, curious.

He said, "Who won yesterday morning? And what about this morning?"

"Oh, I won!" came a laughing voice on the other line. "Is this a bet? Greg--are you there? Don't listen to anything he's telling you--I won, both times!" Another cheerful laugh.

Whitmore glanced at Casey. He then said, "Just remind me, what times were we playing the last two days?"

A pause. "Same schedule, honey. Are you okay?"

"Just humor me. It's a bet."

"I knew it. High, Greg!" came the sing-song, teasing voice of Whitmore's wife. She said, "We always go for a run at six, then go to the court at eight. We leave at ten."

Casey blinked. She supposed when someone could afford a membership to a club like this, one could also afford a leasiurely morning.

But that timeline gave Whitmore a clear alibi for the murders.

She nodded once.

Whitmore noticed the head gesture, and said, "Thanks, dear. See you later tonight!"

And then he hung up, glaring at her, his eyes defiant.

Casey studied Whitmore's face, the colors swirling around him in a haze of truth and sincerity. His alibi appeared solid, but she couldn't dismiss the nagging intuition that lingered in her mind. The strands of evidence were too tightly woven to be easily dismissed as mere coincidence.

"Mr. Whitmore," Casey began, her voice steady and authoritative, "I can't ignore the fact that your jeep is connected to both crime scenes. There must be some explanation."

Whitmore shifted, a ripple of uneasy blue passing through the air. He sighed before responding. "I can understand your skepticism, Agent Bolt. But, as I said earlier, I'm a busy man with a vineyard to run and wine-tasting events to host. My employees often need to use my jeep for various tasks. It's possible one of them could have been involved without my knowledge."

"Is there someone that can confirm your wife's alibi for you?"

"Yes. Cameras at the pickle ball course."

Casey shifted uncomfortably, but then something he'd said caught her attention.

"Your employees," she repeated, her tone sharpening as she focused on the potential connection. "How many of them have access to your jeep?"

Whitmore hesitated, then rubbed his chin thoughtfully. "Well, I'd say about six or seven of them have used the jeep at some point. As for their backgrounds, I can't say I know every detail. We run background checks, of course, but people can change."

"Mr. Whitmore," Casey said, her voice firm with resolve, "I'll need a list of these employees who had access to your jeep. And I will need any information you have on their backgrounds."

He leaned his rifle against the window and crossed his arms now. "I'm not sure I need to give you that information," he said slowly.

She shook her head. "I can request it through other channels."

"Wouldn't be much of a request--is that what you're implying?"

"We're having a conversation here, in this room," she said softly. "In a country club. If we have to do it down at the station, it'll go differently, I'm sure. I'd rather avoid that."

He sighed, rubbing at the bridge of his nose. She could tell he was caving under the pressure.

"Mr. Whitmore," Casey began, her voice steady and in control, "I understand that you don't want to put anyone in the spotlight unfairly. But I need those names. Every detail about them could be a potential lead." She locked eyes with him.

Whitmore hesitated for a moment. He studied her, then sighed, shaking his head. "It'll take me a second to get the information."

He was pulling his phone out, but she mirrored the motion.

"Good," she said coolly. "It'll give me time to check your alibi."

The two of them locked gazes, both of them seemingly sizing up the other as they placed their respective phone calls.

CHAPTER TWENTY

Back at the dimly lit precinct, the small computer room hummed with the steady rhythm of a late-night research session. The clack of keys and swishing sound of sipped coffee did little to assuage Casey's tired eyes.

Shadows stretched across the room, punctuated by the intermittent glow of computer screens and the soft clicking of keyboards. The scent of coffee hung heavy in the air, a comforting aroma that seemed to linger like the last line of defense against exhaustion.

Casey and Nathan were hunched over a cluttered desk, surrounded by paper printouts containing Mr. Whitmore's employee records.

His alibi had checked out. Four hours at a pickleball court--she had to give him credit.

Casey's gloved fingers sifted through the papers, her dark hair pulled back into its usual ponytail.

"Look at this," Nathan said, his voice low and gravelly, eyes narrowing as he examined a document. His rough hands, adorned with knuckle tattoos extended the document towards her.

She shook her head. "Look at the birth year. Too old. No way he'd be able to lift a body into a vat."

"Right." Nathan rubbed at his eyes. "Sorry. Just, tired.."

The clock on the wall ticked away the seconds, its steady rhythm a reminder of the fleeting time.

Casey's gloved fingers traced the edge of a thick stack of papers, her eyes scanning the list of names compiled from Mr. Whitmore's employee records. Each name was like an individual brushstroke, contributing to the abstract tapestry of the case.

"Let's start by checking for criminal records," Nathan suggested, his voice low and steady as he pulled up a database on their shared laptop.

Casey nodded, her eyes narrowing in concentration as she began to type in the first name on the list. She watched as the computer screen flickered to life, the soft glow casting shadows across her face.

The search results began to populate, each name accompanied by a list of any legal infractions.

Nathan leaned in closer, his eyes scanning the screen as he muttered to himself. "Nope, nope, nope...ah, here we go!"

Casey leaned in, her eyes scanning the screen as she read the details of the criminal record.

"Assault with a deadly weapon," she murmured, her eyes flicking back to the list of names. "This could be a lead."

"Who is it?" Nathan asked.

"David Mendoza," Casey replied, her voice quiet.

Nathan nodded, his fingers beginning to fly over the keyboard as he pulled up more information on David Mendoza.

Finally, Nathan let out a low whistle. "This guy is bad news," he said, his voice low and ominous. "Drug trafficking, assault, grand theft auto...the list goes on. How did he pass a background check?"

"Whitmore said all his employees did."

Nathan snorted. "Well... David Mendoza either lied or... no, wait, shit. Here."

"What?"

Nathan tapped the screen. "Mendoza is married to Whitmore's cousin. Family connection. Might not have been so thorough on the background checks."

"Alright, so we've got David Mendoza. Anyone else on the list?"

Here, Nathan frowned. "No... criminal record."

"What is it?" she asked, leaning in to read the second entry.

"There's no known identity."

"How's that?"

"See here? Jimmy Carter."

She blinked. "What, like as in the president?"

Nathan shrugged. "It's the only other person who isn't cleared of a criminal record, but it's because they have *no* record."

"What..."

"No social security. No identity, really."

Casey read the name, Carter, Jimmy. And below it, there was no listed address. No social security. Nothing.

She frowned, wrinkling his nose. "Where do they send his checks?"

Nathan pulled up another document.

"There's an address here," he said.

Casey nodded thoughtfully. "Alright," she murmured. "So let's check out David Mendoza and Mr. Jimmy Carter."

"Split up?"

She sighed, yawning, putting a hand over her mouth and glancing out the window.

She checked her watch. Nearly midnight.

"You tired?" Nathan's voice softened somewhat as he looked at her, a note of concern in his gaze.

"Very," she said.

"Think it can wait until morning?" Nathan asked.

She paused, considering this. The murders happened in the morning. "Don't think we can risk it."

"Fine then. I'll take Mr. Mendoza if you want Carter," Nathan said, already pushing to his feet and reaching for the keys which jangled in his pocket.

Casey nodded, stretching her tired muscles. "Sounds good," she said, rising from her seat. "Meet back here in two hours?"

Nathan nodded, already making his way towards the door. "Got it. Don't fall asleep on me," he teased, a small smile tugging at the corner of his lips.

Casey rolled her eyes, the exhaustion beginning to weigh heavily upon her. "I won't," she said, her voice laced with a small smile.

But the smile faded as she pushed out the door.

Already, multiple women were dead.

If someone had used Whitmore's jeep to stalk their victims, it would've been a member of his company.

Or what if it was a coincidence that his car had been at two crime scenes after all?

Each of these thoughts troubled her, and helped keep sleep at bay as she snatched a coffee mug off the break room's microwave and moved towards the door, double-timing it.

CHAPTER TWENTY ONE

The clock in Casey's car read 11:57 PM as she parked along the curb, the glow of the dashboard casting eerie shadows across her face. The night was moonless, the air thick with the silence only dead hours could offer. She double-checked the address on her phone before stepping out into the darkness, the weight of her FBI badge heavy against her chest.

As she approached the trailer park, the scent of damp earth and old metal permeated the air. Her gloved hands clenched into fists at her sides, a reminder of the barriers she kept between herself and the world. The gloves helped to muffle the sensory onslaught that came with her synesthetic abilities, but they couldn't entirely shield her from the colors that danced in her mind's eye. Tonight, the darkness seemed to take on a deep violet hue, tinged with unease.

Casey found the trailer nestled against the fence at the far end of the park, its paint peeling and windows grimy. She paused for a moment, feeling the tension coil within her like a serpent preparing to strike. It was Jimmy Carter's address, but what would she find inside? She remembered Nathan's voice earlier, rough as gravel, telling her to be careful. She wished he were here now, but he was checking Mendoza.

She murmured to herself, focusing on the sensation of air filling her lungs. It felt cool and crisp, like mint leaves, and for a split second, the colors in her head dulled in intensity.

With renewed determination, Casey crept up to the darkened trailer, wincing as her footsteps crunched on the gravel beneath her. She pressed her body against the cold metal siding, listening intently for any signs of movement within. Hearing nothing, she cautiously peered through one of the murky windows.

Was this the home of a multiple serial killer?

The thought sent shivers down her back.

Backup was on standby, moving in from two miles away, waiting for a call in case she needed them.

At first, the darkness inside seemed impenetrable, but as her eyes adjusted, she began to make out shapes and shadows. An old sofa, a cluttered kitchen counter, and... was that a gun safe in the corner? She squinted, trying to discern more details, but the dim light offered her little. A surge of frustration bubbled up within her, manifesting as sharp, jagged lines of red in her mind.

"Damn it," she whispered through gritted teeth, fighting against the synesthetic sensations that threatened to overwhelm her.

Casey edged around the side of the trailer, her senses tingling with anticipation. The air smelled of rust and damp earth, a vivid contrast to the sterile scentlessness she usually surrounded herself with. As she moved, the texture of the gravel beneath her feet shifted from rough and jagged to smooth and round, like the pebbles on a riverbed.

She noticed evidence of ammunition in the backyard; spent casings littered the ground like fallen leaves, their metallic scent mingling with the sharp tang of shattered glass. It was clear that someone had been taking potshots at the bottles strewn about. The sight sent a shiver down Casey's spine as the colors of danger – dark reds and oranges – danced before her mind's eye. She couldn't help but wonder what other violent tendencies Carter might be harboring.

"Focus," she muttered under her breath, trying to keep her synesthetic distractions at bay. "One step at a time."

With a deep breath, she approached the front door of the trailer, her heart pounding against her ribcage like a trapped bird. Each beat reverberated through her body, the vibrations manifesting as bright flashes of cobalt blue. She steadied her shaking hands, preparing herself for any unexpected encounters. This was it. This was the moment where everything could change.

"Keep your guard up," Casey whispered to herself, her voice barely audible above the hum of insects in the night.

As she reached for the doorknob, a rush of memories flooded her mind - Nathan's reassuring words, her training at Quantico, the countless hours spent poring over case files. All of it had led her here to this small metal box of secrets waiting to be unlocked.

She hesitated as these thoughts crossed her mind, and she muttered to herself.

"Get a grip..."

The exhaustion of a sleepless night was weighing heavily on her now.

As she reached for the doorknob, though, she heard movement.

Before Casey could even turn the handle, the front door slammed open with a force that sent her sprawling backward. The impact rattled her senses, and the world seemed to spin as she hit the ground hard, the air whooshing from her lungs.

"Dammit!" she gasped, struggling to regain her bearings.

Carter emerged from the darkness of the trailer, clad only in tighty-whities that left little to the imagination. He sprinted past Casey without so much as a glance, panic etched across his face, his escape clearly fueled by desperation. As he made a beeline for a dirt bike parked nearby, Casey's instinct to apprehend him kicked into high gear.

"Stop! FBI!" she yelled, scrambling to her feet. But Carter didn't listen. He was already straddling the bike, fumbling with its ignition.

As she took a step forward, the sound of the engine roared to life, drowning out all other noise. Time seemed to slow down as Casey watched Carter revving the dirt bike, preparing to make his getaway.

She moved without conscious thought, her desperation sharpening her focus, driving her body toward action.

Casey moved instinctively, her gloved hands reaching for the garden hose with rapid precision. As Carter revved the dirt bike, she flung the hose towards the spokes like a whip, beads of sweat cascading down her temples.

"Come on," she thought, eyes fixed on the moving target.

The hose slithered through the air, an extension of Casey's determination, before wrapping itself around the speeding vehicle's spokes. The dirt bike wobbled precariously, its engine whirring in protest as the tangled mess brought the machine to a sudden halt.

With a sickening crunch, the front wheel buckled under the strain, sending both Carter and the dirt bike crashing to the ground in a cacophony of metal and curses. The impact reverberated through Casey's body, her synesthetic senses translating the collision into a symphony of color and sensation.

As silence fell over the chaotic aftermath, Casey's heart pounded in her chest, her breaths coming in ragged gasps.

Casey's hands trembled as she approached Carter, her breathing heavy from the adrenaline coursing through her veins. She could almost taste the fear and desperation that emanated from him in thick, dark hues. The thud of her heart pounded like a drum, a metronome driving her forward.

"Stay down!" Casey barked, her voice a mix of command and urgency. She reached into her pocket, producing a pair of handcuffs that gleamed silver under the moonlight.

Carter glared up at her, his eyes smoldering with defiance. "You bitch," he spat, the words slurred by the pain radiating from his battered body.

"Save it for the interrogation room," Casey retorted, her eyes narrowing as she focused on securing his wrists. As the cold metal clicked into place, a strange sense of satisfaction washed over her – but it was short-lived.

The sudden vibration of her phone against her hip jolted Casey out of her single-minded pursuit. She hesitated for a moment, torn between maintaining control over Carter and answering the call.

She fumbled with her free hand to retrieve the phone. Finally, she managed to press it to her ear, her voice strained as she spoke. "Bolt here."

"Casey, it's Nathan."

"Is everything okay?" she asked, trying to keep her voice steady.

His tone was urgent, tinged with a mix of relief and concern. "We've just cleared Mendoza. He has an alibi."

Her breath hitched in her chest as the weight of his words settled upon her. She could almost taste the tangy bitterness of disappointment, the flavor dancing on the tip of her tongue. If Mendoza was innocent, then that left only one person: Carter.

She glanced down at the tighty-whity-wearing suspect.

"Are you sure?" she asked, her thoughts racing like wildfire.

"Positive," he replied. "His crew chief confirmed he was working an early shift at the warehouse during the time of the murder."

The silence that followed was deafening, filled with unspoken questions and lingering uncertainties. Casey's gaze fell on Carter once more, studying the sweat-slicked skin of his half-naked body, the defiant glint in his eyes. Her fingers twitched within their gloves, itching for answers.

"Then that leaves only my guy," she said, steel filling her voice as resolve crystallized within her. "I'm bringing him in for questioning."

"Be careful, Casey," Nathan warned, his concern for her safety evident even across the distance. "He's dangerous."

"I will," she promised.

As she hung up the call, her focus returned to the task at hand. Carter's narrowed eyes followed her every move, like those of a cornered animal. She knew that beneath his calm facade, he must have been calculating, plotting his next desperate attempt at freedom.

"Your turn to talk, Carter," Casey said, her voice low as she hoisted him to his feet. "You're coming with me."

He sneered. "I've got nothing to say."

"Time will tell," she replied, tightening her grip on his arm as they began their slow march towards her car. In the back of her mind, colors swirled and blended, weaving a tangled web of emotions: fear, determination, and the ever-present tinge of doubt.

Carter's tighty-whities glowed in the moonlight as Casey led him towards her car, his handcuffs clinking with each step. The trailer park remained eerily silent, save for the distant hum of cicadas and the occasional rustle of wind through the trees. She maintained a firm grip on his arm, her eyes never leaving him despite the whirlwind of thoughts threatening to consume her.

"Watch your step," she said, her voice steady and professional, though the exhaustion gnawed at the edges of her words.

She pushed him to the car, and he tensed like a coiled rattlesnake, shooting a quick, panicked glance over his shoulder in her direction, his eyes widening.

"Come on, now," she coaxed.

He stared at her, breathing heavily, clearly under the influence of some substance.

"I..." he shook his head, closing his eyes as if shutting out the light. "I..."

He trailed off, uncertain what to say next.

She could feel her own nerves now sparking like alarms. Was this their killer?

She shivered.

Morning was on the way.

If they'd gotten it wrong, then another woman's life was in danger during the wee hours of the coming morning.

CHAPTER TWENTY TWO

It was a heavy heart that she found herself back at the motel.

Carter had lawyered up.

The lawyer had promptly demanded a wellness check from the judge.

And so they had to wait until morning.

Casey was seething.

She muttered under her breath as the keys to the motel jangled in her hand. They didn't *have* until morning.

If they were wrong about Carter...

But she forced the thoughts aside, pausing as the door opened, her hand resting on the handle.

She kept the door closed, though ajar, closing her eyes as well, and allowing her deep breaths to calm her mind.

"Review the facts," she murmured to herself.

Whitmore's Jeep had been spotted at two of the murder locations. But what if she'd been wrong about the tread?

No. She shook her head. Her gift was a burden at times, but it wasn't inaccurate.

The jeep had been at both.

She paused, tilting her head. Whitmore had an iron-clad alibi. But some of his employees sometimes borrowed his jeep, though they weren't registered to do so.

She sighed.

Carter had assaulted her.

It made sense. They had the right guy, didn't they?

She shook her head.

"Won't know until morning," she muttered at no one but the watchful moon.

Casey, her mind heavy with the day's events, pushed open the door to her motel room and stepped inside. The air was stale and thick with the scent of a thousand weary travelers come and gone before her. She felt the weight of exhaustion bearing down on her shoulders, as if she were Atlas, condemned to hold up the sky for all eternity.

The room itself seemed to be an extension of her fatigue. It was small and cramped, the wallpaper peeling away in large swaths from the walls like desiccated leaves. A single, flickering bulb dangled precariously from the ceiling, casting long shadows across the faded carpet that had once been a vibrant crimson but now resembled the color of dried blood.

In one corner stood a battered dresser, its chipped veneer revealing the tired wood beneath; the mirror above it was cracked and fogged with age. Opposite the dresser, a threadbare armchair sagged beneath the weight of invisible ghosts, its green fabric worn thin and shiny in places from years of use.

A queen-sized bed dominated the center of the room, the sheets rumpled and stained, the pillows flat and lumpy. Casey could almost feel the dust mites crawling through the mattress, their microscopic bodies joining the chorus of unseen presences that haunted the dimly lit space.

Closing the door behind her, she leaned against it for a moment, closing her eyes and taking a deep breath. In the darkness behind her eyelids, she saw flashes of color.

With a sigh, she straightened her posture and unzipped her jacket, the sound echoing through the room like the peel of distant thunder. Her gloves remained on her hands, a barrier against the motel room's oppressive atmosphere. She moved to the center of the room, feeling it close in around her like a suffocating embrace.

The dim light flickered above her, casting shadows that seemed to dance and writhe with a life of their own. The darkness was alive, pulsing with secrets, threats lurking just beyond her reach.

In the wake of the day's events, Casey stood in the center of her motel room, its worn-out appearance and dim lighting echoing her own exhaustion. Shadows clung to the edges of the space, their tendrils reaching out as if trying to grasp her. The wallpaper, faded and peeling, formed grotesque shapes that seemed to undulate with every flicker of the lone bulb overhead.

Casey took a deep breath, steadying herself. She slowly removed her gloves, feeling the air on her fingertips like a soft caress. As she placed them on the small table by the bed, she closed her eyes for a moment, allowing the ritual to ground her amidst the storm of emotions threatening to consume her.

Her phone buzzed in her pocket, jolting her from the brief respite. She hesitated, then pulled it out and glanced at the screen. A reminder from earlier. The same message she'd ignored. A text message from

Zach stared back at her, its contents simple but loaded with implications. Her thumb hovered over the screen, torn between replying and ignoring him.

"Come on, Casey," she whispered to herself.

She let out a frustrated groan, pacing the confines of the cramped room. The scuffed wooden floor creaked beneath her feet, the sound grating against her nerves. Could she afford to let Zach in, knowing full well the potential dangers he might bring along with him? Or would she be damning herself to an even greater loneliness by shutting him out?

"Damn it," she muttered, her voice barely audible above the hum of the ancient air conditioner. She knew she couldn't make this decision lightly, but her exhaustion weighed heavily on her, clouding her thoughts and amplifying her fears.

"Focus," she told herself, taking a deep breath. She could feel the colors swirling in her mind, each one vying for her attention as she tried to gain control over her synesthesia. Finally, she steeled her resolve, and with trembling fingers, began to type out a response to Zach's message.

Her heart pounded in her chest, a mix of anticipation and anxiety coursing through her veins. Would she regret this decision? Only time will tell. But at least for now, she had made her choice, and that was a step forward.

A soft exhale escaped Casey's lips as she stared down at her phone, her thumb hovering over the screen. The dim light in her motel room cast a faint, otherworldly glow on her face, highlighting the deep lines of exhaustion etched into her features. Her heart raced with trepidation, each erratic beat painting vivid colors across her mind's eye.

"Hi. Doing alright. Hbu?" she typed hesitantly, the word seeming far too simple for the weight it carried. Her fingers trembled slightly before pressing send, and a wave of vulnerability washed over her. The decision to respond felt like an admission of weakness, a concession to her own loneliness. Yet, despite her misgivings, she couldn't deny the sense of relief that came from reaching out, as if she were grasping at a lifeline.

"Hey, Cas. Good to hear from you. Want to meet up?" Zach's reply appeared almost immediately, the words glowing brightly against the darkened screen. A sudden surge of anxiety threatened to overwhelm her, her thoughts racing with all the possible consequences of seeing him again.

113

The temptation was strong; the prospect of reconnecting with someone who knew her so well was undeniably appealing. At the same time, she couldn't shake the feeling of uncertainty gnawing at the edges of her consciousness, warning her that there might be more at stake than she could anticipate.

"Where?" she found herself typing, the question slipping out as if it had a will of its own. The seconds following felt like an eternity as she awaited his response, the silence between them becoming a cacophony of unspoken emotions and fears.

"Let's go somewhere new. I'll text you the address tomorrow. Sound good?"

"Maybe," she replied, her pulse quickening with a mix of excitement and apprehension.

Not a commitment. Why. A hedge.

She shook her head in disgust.

The anticipation that filled her chest felt like a tangible weight, making it difficult to breathe as she lay back on the worn-out bedspread. She closed her eyes, attempting to quiet her racing thoughts and find solace in sleep. Yet, even as her body craved rest, her mind refused to relent, consumed by the decision she had made.

She couldn't sleep.

Her adrenaline was surging.

She pushed off the bed again, cursing under her breath.

The dim light from the bedside lamp cast elongated shadows on the peeling wallpaper, giving the cramped motel room an eerie, unsettling atmosphere. Casey paced back and forth in front of the window, her footsteps muffled by the threadbare carpet beneath her feet. Her gloved hands clenched and unclenched at her sides as she tried to focus her thoughts on the potential consequences of meeting Zach.

"Is this really a good idea?" she whispered aloud, her voice barely audible above the hum of the air conditioner.

Her mind raced with memories of the past, the wounds still raw and unhealed. Betrayal had left its mark on her once before, and the thought of opening herself up to that kind of pain again was almost too much to bear. But there was something about Zach that made her want to take the risk, something that called to her like a siren's song.

Her synesthetic senses flared, colors swirling around her like a chaotic tempest as she tried to make sense of her emotions. The dull beige of the walls bled into the sickly green of the stained curtains, mirroring her own feelings of unease and uncertainty.

She just shook her head in frustration, ignoring the phone and plopping onto the bed.

Sleep remained elusive. Minutes ticked by, but she still lay there, encumbered by the great gift of consciousness.

As Casey tossed and turned in her sleep, the sheets twisted around her body like a serpent, constricting her every movement. Her dreams were a whirlwind of disjointed images and sensations, echoing the turmoil building within her mind.

In one moment, she found herself standing alone in a dimly lit alley, the oppressive darkness closing in on her from all sides. A figure emerged from the shadows, its face obscured by the darkness. A voice called out to her, barely audible above the pounding rain that soaked her to the bone.

"Casey!" The voice strained with urgency, but as she tried to focus on the face behind it, the figure dissolved into a mist, leaving only the faint echo of the name.

Casey's heart raced as she stumbled through the labyrinth of narrow streets, desperately seeking answers and feeling the weight of an unseen danger lurking behind every corner. Her gloved hands reached out to touch the cold brick walls, each sensation seeping into her synesthetic senses like drops of ink in water, creating vibrant colors and patterns that threatened to overwhelm her.

In another scene, Casey stood before a cracked mirror, her reflection staring back at her with hollow, haunted eyes. As she watched, the image began to distort, stretching and twisting until it was no longer recognizable. A guttural scream tore from her throat, but the sound was swallowed by the suffocating silence that enveloped her.

"Please," she pleaded, her voice trembling with fear. "Tell me what's happening."

Her dream-self reached out, attempting to grasp the fragments of truth hidden within the chaos, but they slipped through her fingers like fine sand, scattering into the void. The harder she tried to hold onto them, the more they evaded her.

"Casey," a familiar voice whispered, suddenly close to her ear. She recognized it as Nathan's, offering comfort amidst the storm of uncertainty raging within her. "You're stronger than this. Trust yourself."

The words seemed to anchor her, providing a brief respite from the tempest of her emotions. But as quickly as it came, Nathan's voice faded away, leaving her once again adrift in the darkness.

"Wait!" she cried out, reaching for the connection that was slipping away. "I need you!"

Her fingers brushed against something solid—a lifeline amidst the chaos—but just as she tried to grasp it, it slipped away like smoke, leaving her cold and alone.

As Casey drifted through the sea of fractured images and sensations, she felt the undercurrents of fear and apprehension tighten their grip on her subconscious, threatening to pull her under completely. The decision to meet Zach loomed above her like a specter, casting its shadow over every aspect of her dreams.

"Is this the right choice?" Casey's thoughts spiraled, but no answer was forthcoming, as the ever-shifting dreamscape continued to evade her grasp.

Tomorrow morning, she'd speak with Carter.

She wouldn't wait.

Not now.

The dreams were uncertainty--mirroring her own.

She was't certain.

Was Carter their killer?

And if not... would she wake to find another body?

CHAPTER TWENTY THREE

Morning came none too quickly, and Casey double-timed from the parking lot.

She barely shared a nod with Nathan where Hayes was leaning against the outside of the precinct, munching on some sunflower seeds in his ever diligent attempts to stave off an old smoking habit.

Side by side, they moved rapidly down the second hall.

"Hear anything from Carter's lawyer?" Nathan asked.

She didn't glance over, but simply said, stifling a yawn, "We're greenlit."

"Good."

She nodded once.

Casey and Nathan strode into the cold interrogation room. The smell of stale sweat, body odor, and disinfectant walloped them like a fist to the face. Slumped in a metal chair and wearing an oversized, bright orange jumpsuit was Jimmy Carter.

No longer in his tighty-whities, he looked utterly exhausted, bruised around his eyes from lack of sleep. His clothes were disheveled, his hair greasy and unkempt. The only splash of color on Carter's person was the bright blue tattoo of a dragon that curled around his forearm.

Carter glared up at the two agents, tiredness evident in his bloodshot eyes.

"I hear you been complaining all night," Nathan said, gruff as ever.

Carter snorted. "This cell you stuck me in is awful. Hardly any room to stretch. And that cot—felt like sleeping on rocks."

Nathan pulled up a chair opposite the suspect and leaned forward, his eyes narrowing. "Don't care much."

"Yeah? Why don't I tell my lawyer that."

"You tell her whatever the hell you want," Nathan said, tapping his fingers against the back of the metal chair. "You hit my partner here with a door."

Carter glanced at Casey, then back at Nathan. "She your girlfriend or somethin?"

"Shut up, asshole."

Carter smirked. "She is, huh? You screwing the bitch?"

Casey didn't react, and instead she placed a hand on Nathan's shoulder.

He could be tempermental and unpredictable at times, and there wasn't a doubt that Nathan would do everything he could to get back at Carter for such a comment, but Hayes was also a professional.

He knew when a suspect was trying to get a rise out of him.

"You'd like me to black an eye, chip a tooth," Hayes said with a smirk, leaning back. "Wouldn't you? No, bud. You're gonna be getting real used to cots like that. Trust me."

"I don't trust pigs."

Casey sat down as well now, and ignoring the exchange, she cleared her throat and looked up.

Nathan glanced in her direction as she said, "Let's talk about your whereabouts the past few mornings between 4 and 6am." Her voice was stern, uncompromising.

Carter grumbled to himself as he stared at the table, avoiding eye contact with Nathan or Casey.

"I already told that other cop; I was home in bed," he replied with a heavy sigh.

"Anyone that can verify that?" Casey asked.

"No," he replied petulantly.

"Well, that's convenient," Nathan said, folding his arms across his chest.

Carter slouched a little lower in his chair and glared at the agents.

"You know, I'm getting real tired of this," he said. "I didn't do nothin' wrong."

Nathan sighed and shook his head. "Jimmy, we're gonna need better than that. Why don't you just tell us the truth and save us all some time? Did you borrow Whitmore's Jeep?"

"Did I... what the hell? That asshole been saying I did?"

"Did you?" Casey doubled down.

"Hell no."

Casey shrugged, and then, remembering the door to the face last night, she lied. "You were seen driving his Jeep."

Carter hesitated, as if sizing her up. Then he leaned back, shrugging nonchalantly.

"So what if I did. Aint a crime."

"No," Casey said slowly, her face impassive, not revealing that he'd just shown his hand by confirming he'd borrowed the jeep. "But..." she trailed off. "Murder is. And the Jeep was seen at two crime scenes."

She leaned forward, "Not to mention, Mr. Carter, you're using a fake name."

"Bullshit."

"You are. No social security."

"My real name."

"Jimmy Carter?" Nathan said with a roll of his eyes. "A bit on the nose, no?"

"It's my name," he repeated more adamantly.

Casey shrugged. "Either way, why don't you tell us who you really are."

"I told you already, it is my name. I never registered nor nothing. I was born in the mountains. Like it matters to you." He jutted his chin out, sneering at her.

"Doesn't mean you wouldn't have a birth certificate."

"Does if you ain't ask for one. Born at home."

Casey shook her head. "So how come Whitmore hired you?"

"Whitmore? He doesn't care. I work hard. Besides, last night was your fault. You're the one who sneaked up on me and all. Thought you were there to kill me."

"And when I told you I was FBI?" she retorted.

He shrugged. "Couldn't hear you."

He leaned back now, closing his eyes and stifling a yawn. "This really what we gotta do?" he said. "Seems a waste of time."

Casey and Nathan shared a look.

Carter slumped in his chair, head lolling to the side as if he dozed. Nathan slammed his hands down on the table.

"Wake up, Carter!" he barked. "We're not done with you yet."

Carter jerked awake, eyes bleary. "Wha...I told you everything already," he mumbled.

"Oh, we're just getting started," Nathan said, his voice dangerously low. He began peppering Carter with rapid-fire questions. "When's the last time you drove Whitmore's jeep?"

"Dunno."

"Have you ever used wine as a weapon?"

"W-what the hell?"

"Do you like drowning things, Carter?"

"Hell no! I hate the water!"

Carter squirmed under the barrage, his answers hesitant and confused. Casey studied him closely, searching for any glimmer of deception. But all she saw was a disoriented, frightened man way out of his depth. Her doubts solidified.

119

She'd been worried about Carter.

Worried, because he'd been such a frightened rabbit. And now... here, bleary-eyed, exhausted.

Was he the sort to hunt someone down in the wee hours of the morning?

This man didn't seem like a threat.

He seemed like a joke.

She shook her head at the harsh characterization and massaged the bridge of her nose.

"What were you doing yesterday morning," she said.

"I told you, sleeping."

"But no one can verify it," Nathan retorted, his tone carrying disbelief.

"Believe what you want."

Casey watched him closely. Blues, greens, some reds.

Anger, anxiety...

No guilt. Was he just belligerent because he disliked cops?

That didn't mean he was guilty of murder.

She hesitated, then pushed to her feet, pacing back and forth.

He watched her move, scowling as she did.

Casey bit her lower lip, studying the man where he sat sleep-deprived in his orange jumpsuit.

And suddenly, her phone began to ring.

She glanced down. An unknown number. She frowned, shooting a look at Nathan, and inching up an eyebrow as if to ask *you got this*?

Nathan gave her a quick nod.

She turned and, lifting the phone, moved hastily out into the hall.

"Hello? Agent Bolt," she said.

"Holy shit!" came the voice, shouting. "What the hell did you do with my wife!"

She paused, and it took a second, but then she recognized the voice.

"Whitmore?" she said.

He was hyperventilating on the other line. Breathing rapidly.

"Whitmore, what's wrong? Is your wife okay?"

"No, she isn't--you assholes arrested her!"

Casey frowned, standing still. "No... we..." she trailed off, and her eyes widened. "Whitmore, listen to me now. We had nothing to do with it. Where are you? What happened? Tell me *right now*."

120

CHAPTER TWENTY FOUR

Casey paced the hallway outside the interrogation room intently as she listened to the phone call.

She could hear him breathing heavily on the other line, and so she said, as firmly as she could, "Whitmore, you need to tell me what happened."

The country club wine-supplier took a shaky breath, trying to compose himself as he recounted the events. "I came home from work, and the front door was wide open. I called out for Gabbie, but there was no answer. I searched the house, and she's just... gone." A pause, a swallow. "Did you arrest her?" he demanded.

"I told you--we had nothing to do with this. Tell me more. I need specifics. Was anything disturbed or out of place? Any signs of forced entry?" she asked, her voice steady despite the growing concern that threatened to consume her.

"Uh, the living room... it looks like there was a struggle. Things are knocked over, some broken glass," Whitmore replied, his voice cracking. "I didn't see any signs of forced entry, though."

"Whitmore, I need you to stay calm and listen carefully," Casey instructed, her mind already leaping ahead, connecting the dots, but she kept her tone calm. "Look along the floors for me. Anything?"

A small gasp. Then, Whitmore's voice trembled as he continued, "There's... there's blood on the floor, just a few drops. And Gabbie's favorite vase – shattered. I knew something was wrong the moment I stepped in, but I didn't want to believe it." His breathing hitched, the distress evident in every word.

Casey's synesthetic mind painted vivid colors of fear and urgency as she listened to Whitmore's description. She could almost taste the metallic tang of blood and feel the sharp edges of broken glass beneath her gloved fingertips. This had become all too familiar, and she needed to act fast to prevent another tragedy.

"Stay where you are, Whitmore. Don't touch anything," Casey instructed, her voice firm with determination. "I'm on my way."

"Please hurry," Whitmore whispered, his voice barely audible.

"One last thing, are you just getting home now?" she said.

"Yes. I stayed overnight at the club. Couldn't drive."

Casey huffed in frustration. If that was the case, then their current suspect might still have been involved. Nathan had to continue the interrogation, but someone had to tend to this new situation.

As she ended the call, Casey's heart raced, the adrenaline surging through her veins like liquid fire. Her thoughts swirled with hues of red and gold, each synesthetic sensation propelling her forward. Time was slipping away, and Gabbie's life hung in the balance.

With practiced efficiency, Casey grabbed her jacket from the back of the chair in the breakroom at the end of the hall; she shrugged it on, her movements swift and purposeful. The cold fabric against her skin grounded her, focusing her senses on the task at hand. She couldn't afford any distractions.

Her footsteps echoed down the dimly lit hallway, the sound punctuated by the urgency that pulsed within her.

She glanced down the hall only briefly, but Nathan had to continue the interrogation. Maybe their suspect had kidnapped Gabbie and was holding her somewhere. Maybe that's why he'd run...

Or maybe they were almost out of time.

She sent a quick text as she doubled her pace, moving towards the exit. "Send me a picture of Gabbie," she texted.

She reached her car, keys in hand, just as her phone buzzed in response, each one of her steps urgent.

The glow of Casey's phone screen illuminated her face as she opened the message from Whitmore. The woman in the picture was strikingly beautiful, with large, expressive eyes that spoke a thousand unspoken words and a smile that lit up the dark confines of the car.

Casey studied Gabbie's face more closely, her synesthetic senses painting colors around the edges of the image. She noticed the way Gabbie's eyes seemed to dance with an internal fire, the deep blue hue swirling with flecks of gold and green. As she took in these details, something struck her – a sense of familiarity that sent chills down her spine.

She stared at the image, pausing only briefly.

Then, she flipped to the images of their previous victims--including the cold cases.

She drew up the pictures of the other women, and stared.

At first, it might have been hard to see the resemblance.

But after a bit, if one studied the faces...

A similar curve to the jawline, similar upturned noses. Similar smiles.

The women looked like one another.

She shook her head, biting her lip.

How had she *missed* this at first?

But it was like Gabbie was the final piece. Other parts of the women's faces were similar but not identical. Each victim seemed to possess only *some* of the other victims' traits.

It was only while staring at them collectively that it became apparent.

She muttered under her breath, checked the address Whitmore had sent, and flung herself into the car, peeling out of the parking lot.

As she sped away from the precinct towards the scene of the abduction, she placed a quick call to Nathan.

He answered on the second ring.

"You coming back in here?" Nathan said. "I think we might be getting near a confession."

"Really?"

"Well... maybe. He's exhausted."

"I'm not there, Nathan. Had to leave."

"W-what, wait, huh?"

"I got a call from Whitmore. His wife's missing. I need to follow up on that lead," Casey explained, the urgency in her voice palpable. "I'll fill you in when I can."

"You need backup? What the hell? Where are you?"

"Stay with him. Figure out if he had anything to do with it. Whitmore didn't get back until this morning."

"Shit."

"So what about you?"

"En route."

"Casey. Wait, hang on."

But Casey didn't respond. She ended the call and tossed the phone onto the passenger seat, keeping her eyes on the road as she picked up speed.

The road ahead stretched out like a dark, endless ribbon, the headlights of her car illuminating the way. Casey pushed her foot down on the accelerator, the speedometer climbing higher and higher. She had a gut feeling that time was running out, and she couldn't afford to waste a single second.

As she neared the address Whitmore had sent her, Casey's heart pounded in her chest. The colors around her grew darker, as if the world knew the gravity of the situation. She had to keep her focus, had to be the calm in the storm that was brewing.

She pulled up to the house, her eyes scanning the area for any signs of movement. The street was quiet, the only sound the distant hum of the city. She exited her car, her senses on high alert as she approached the front door.

It was unlocked.

Whitmore stood in the front room, head in his hands, still wearing that expensive suit she'd seen him in.

Under the light of morning, he looked more exhausted and wrinkled.

When he looked up, his face crested from hope to sheer disappointment.

"Anything?" he said quickly.

Casey shook her head. For a moment, neither of them exchanged any words--the silence seemed suitable to the moment.

Whitmore shuffled aside as if to give her a better look at the living room.

He'd been right; it showed signs of a conflict.

Casey's eyes scanned the room, taking in every detail with a practiced eye. The overturned coffee table, the shattered vase, the ripped curtains – all of it pointed towards a struggle. They needed to find Gabbie before it was too late, before she became the next victim in this sick game.

"We need to get started on finding her," Casey said, her voice low and urgent. "Can you think of anyone who might have a grudge against you or your wife, anyone who might want to hurt her?"

Whitmore shook his head, his eyes filled with tears. "No, Casey. We've never had any enemies. We keep to ourselves. Gabbie is a good woman – she doesn't deserve this."

Casey placed a reassuring hand on his shoulder, squeezing gently. "We'll find her, Whitmore. I promise."

But even as she said the words, a part of her wondered if they were too late.

Already, sunlight streamed through the windows near the torn curtains.

The last two victims had been found in the morning.

She shivered, shaking her head in frustration.

She paced back and forth now, saying, "We looked into your employees. Are you sure you gave us a list of everyone involved?" She stared at him.

124

He blinked, hesitant. "Y-yes. Involved..."

"In the business," she said quickly. "Everyone who would've had access to your jeep."

He nodded adamantly.

She frowned, shaking her head. "Did your wife leave any clue? Any message?" she said quickly.

"N-no. How... what's happening? Is she... is she..." he trailed off, biting his lip as if he couldn't bear to finish the sentence.

She glossed past the unspoken question, and instead of continuing, she began to move through the living room, glancing side to side.

Her eyes flitted over a coffee table, then towards the hall.

She hesitated. A streak of red on the wall leading down the hall.

"Where does this lead?" she said.

"The bedrooms! And... and a bathroom! But I checked. No one's in the bedroom. Or bathroom."

Casey just nodded but approached the doors at the end of the hall, one on the left, the other on the right.

She opened the left door first, and stepped inside. The bedroom was dark, but a sliver of light streamed in from the window on the opposite wall. She stepped forward, her eyes adjusting to the darkness. There was a bed neatly made with an old quilt draped across it. It looked like someone had slept in it recently, but there was no sign of Gabbie.

The window was locked tight, and Casey could see nothing outside except for a few trees swaying in the gentle breeze.

She sighed and moved towards the other door on the right. The bathroom.

She pushed open the door, and then she went still, frowning.

The mirror was shattered.

She hesitated only briefly, glancing along the the rest of the bathroom's cramped floor. Shattered glass scattered over the tiles.

It looked as if someone had kicked around the glass and then left in a hurry.

Casey's heart sank.

She stepped back out of the bathroom, her mind racing with thoughts.

She was missing something. She could feel it.

She glanced along the walls, eyes narrowed, and then she hesitated only briefly.

She'd spotted the blood on the wall towards the entrance to the hall. She approached this section again, all too aware of Whitmore watching her every move.

But she was focused now. Her own emotions were casting odd colors and scents. She could detect the fragrance of Whitmore's cologne, but this was to be expected in his home.

She shook her head, and as she did, she spotted something odd.

A nail jutting from the wall.

She frowned, approached.

The nail was alone, but there was a dust pattern above the stain of blood. A pattern of a rectangle. She hesitated, and then tapped the empty space.

"What used to hang here?" she asked.

He stared, stammered. "I... a.. a family picture."

She looked at him. "Who was in it?"

"Just me and my wife and our son."

She nodded slowly. "Why would someone take a family picture?" And why would someone shatter a mirror? she thought. Not Gabbie. No--whoever had done it was stronger than that.

Someone who'd raged against the glass.

And someone who'd stolen a family photo.

Or...

Maybe not stolen...

Her eyes widened a bit. And she peered along the back of a television table.

She leaned forward, and there, spotted a flicker of glass.

A shattered picture frame.

"Here!" she said sharply. "Help me move this!" she snapped her fingers, and Whitmore came rapidly towards her, taking long strides, his face pale.

"What is it?" he asked.

But she just waited as he began to pull the table away from the wall.

And then she saw it.

The family photo, the glass shattered and torn. And there, the son's face was ripped apart.

Casey felt a chill run through her body.

She reached out to carefully take the frame from where it rested, studying it closely. All she could make out were bits of paper where Whitmore's son's face should have been, as if someone had taken great pains to ensure that no one would ever know what he looked like again.

She glanced up at Whitmore, who seemed lost in thought, his eyes distant and troubled. He looked like someone who'd seen too much, like someone who'd experienced far more than anyone should have to bear.

It was clear that whoever had done this had wanted to erase something from his life - or maybe even from history itself - but why? What could be so important or so damaging that it needed to be erased?

And why the son?

The wife's smiling face was as beautiful as the photo Whitmore had provided, though wrinkled from the abuse the photo had received.

Casey stared.

Her mind whirring.

Someone had shattered the mirror. Had defaced the photo...

Her eyes widened, if only imperceptibly. "Can I see a photo of your son?"

"I... what?"

"Your son. I need to see a photo of him. How old is he?"

"In this picture? Twenty, maybe..."

"Now?"

"Early twenties."

"Picture, please," she said. And she snapped her fingers again, since the auditory cue had prompted him to action when moving the TV table.

He blinked once, but then with trembling fingers reached into his pocket to pull out his phone.

He scrolled through his photos and selected one of his son. Casey leaned over his shoulder to get a better look. The boy in the photo was handsome, with a bright smile and piercing blue eyes. Casey studied the photo for a moment longer.

"What's his name?"

"Gregory."

"Greg?"

"No, Gregory."

Casey nodded. "Does he have any enemies? Anyone who'd want to hurt him?"

She stared at the photo.

"N-no... No. I mean... he had a DUI a while back. But other than that, he's a good kid."

"Anything else?"

"What?"

"What's the part you're not telling me?" she said.

"Nothing!"

"Sir..."

And then she trailed off, the pieces swirling about in her mind, slowly clicking into place.

A jeep that had been borrowed from Whitmore...

Victims that all looked alike. A broken mirror. A shattered picture. The wine business...

Her eyes suddenly widened.

"It's revenge," she whispered.

"What's that?"

"Against himself."

Whitmore was staring at her as if she'd gone mad.

But her heart pounded fervently, and she was nodding to herself rapidly. "Yes," she whispered. "I think I know what's going on," she said slowly. "Someone is trying to erase your son from history. They've shattered the mirror and defaced the photo to make sure no one knows what he looks like."

Whitmore's face went pale. "But why? Who would want to do that?"

She felt distracted now, as if there were a taste just at the tip of her tongue, but she couldn't place it. Casey replied. "Do you have any enemies? Anyone who might want to harm your family?"

Whitmore shook his head. "No, not that I can think of. We've always kept to ourselves, tried to stay out of trouble."

Casey nodded, deep in thought. "We need to find your son, Mr. Whitmore. Do you have any idea where he might be?"

Whitmore shook his head again. "I haven't heard from him in weeks. He's been traveling, doing some backpacking in Europe. But he always checks in with us, lets us know he's okay."

"Mr. Whitmore, I'm going to need you to give me your son's full name and any information you have about..."

But she paused. Yes... yes, it made sense.

"Does your son have anger issues, Mr. Whitmore?" she said suddenly.

"I beg your pardon!"

"Does he work for your company? Does he use the jeep? His name wasn't on the list of employees you gave me. NO DUIs showed up on any of our records.

He gaped at her, hesitated, mouth unhinged, then closed his mouth again.

"What are you implying?"

"He looks an awful lot like your wife, doesn't he?" she mused, staring at the photo still visible in Whitmore's trembling hand.

Now, the pieces were clicking into place.

Someone hated themselves... broke a mirror. Wanted revenge against... People in the wine industry?

"How's your relationship with your son, sir?"

He stared at her.

"I... I..."

He targeted people who looked like his own mother. Like himself. Shit...

"Sir, what's your son's phone number?"

"Slow down and answer my damn questions!" he bellowed.

But she ignored him now, shaking her head, feeling her nerves jangling.

Yes... yes, she was right. It was Gregory Whitmore.

The real killer... he wasn't in Europe. He was here.

And he'd taken his own mother captive--he'd been killing women involved in his father's industry.

"I need his phone number!" she snapped. "Right now!"

CHAPTER TWENTY FIVE

Casey gripped the steering wheel tightly, her gloves slick against the leather.

The morning sunlight had given way to cloud cover.

The cloud cover had given to storming weather while she'd sped through city streets, but now as she headed towards the mountains, tracking Gregory Whitmore's phone, the storm had intensified, its howling wind and rain a cacophony around her.

The find-my-phone app Whitmore had reluctantly provided gave a steady red dot on her screen, and she stared at it as if her life depended on it.

She put on an extra burst of speed, tempting the slick road with how rapidly she tore through the streets.

She squinted through the windshield, watching as the dark clouds churned ominously above the Washington mountains. The wipers could barely keep up with the deluge pouring from the sky. Her GPS guided her deeper into the heart of the storm, towards the location where Gregory Whitmore's phone kept pinging.

He wasn't in Europe.

Backup was on its way, but the storm had slowed them.

As Casey navigated the treacherous mountain road, lightning illuminated the landscape in sudden, violent bursts. A flash of electric blue erupted across the sky, casting eerie shadows on the rugged terrain. The thunder rumbled, a deep and foreboding growl that resonated within her chest.

The relentless downpour painted the world in shades of gray, but Casey's synesthesia transformed the scene into a symphony of color. The cascading raindrops danced like silver ribbons, while the low rumble of thunder vibrated in hues of midnight blue and indigo. It should have been beautiful, but there was no time for appreciation – not when lives were at stake.

Despite the danger posed by the storm, Casey pressed on, her foot heavier on the gas pedal than it should have been. She couldn't shake the feeling that she was running out of time. The weight of responsibility pressed down on her shoulders, tightening like a vice around her chest.

Just as another jagged bolt of lightning cleaved the sky, Casey recognized the location of the GPS.

Shit.

The country club.

He'd taken his victim to the country club; she recalled the country club she visited the previous night: opulent chandeliers hanging from the ceiling, taxidermy animals frozen in eternal vigilance on the walls, the swirling wine glasses full of aged burgundy. That world seemed so far away from the tempest engulfing her now, yet it held the key to unraveling the twisted web she found herself entangled in.

The storm continued to rage around her, the torrential rain blurring the lines between reality and the vivid colors painted by her own senses. The road ahead seemed to stretch on endlessly, but Casey knew she couldn't afford to waver in her resolve.

"Come on, come on," she muttered under her breath, urging the car forward through the storm, her eyes scanning the darkness for any sign of her whereabouts. Her thoughts raced, piecing together the fragments of evidence she had gathered, building a chilling picture of the Whitmore family and the secrets they harbored.

Gregory, the son – charming, cunning, and potentially more dangerous than anyone had realized. As the storm raged around her, Casey couldn't shake the gnawing suspicion that he held the key to his mother's disappearance and possible murder.

"Is it too late?" she whispered, her voice barely audible above the howling wind.

"Dammit," she muttered, her jaw set in a grim line as she stared into the stormy darkness.

She knew she needed to do something - anything - to buy more time, to keep Gregory from executing his twisted plan.

She hadn't wanted to contact him. She didn't want him startled.

But now...

No, time was of the essence, and she needed to stall him.

Without hesitation, she reached for her phone, her fingers flying over the screen as she dialed Gregory's number. She knew she had to act fast to keep him occupied.

"Come on, come on," she urged, the ringing tone cutting through the cacophony of the storm. "Pick up, you bastard."

No one answered.

Casey resisted the urge to scream, and in so doing, nearly veered off the road.

Her front tires slipped, and he fought to regain control of the car. The wheels spun uselessly, throwing up a spray of mud and water. Casey gritted her teeth, her knuckles white as she clenched the steering wheel, turning into the spin, the re-righting the car before she plunged off the road.

A wreck wouldn't do at all.

Not now. Not when she was this close.

With trembling fingers, she dialed again.

One ring... two... three...

And then.

"What?" short, curt, angry.

She kept her tone pleasant. The goal was to delay, not confront. "Gregory Whitmore?"

"Yeah. Who's this?"

"I'm..." she hesitated, then pressed on with the lie. "I'm calling on behalf of your father. I'm afraid there's been an accident."

"Huh." He didn't add anything else.

She pressed on; at least he was still on the line.

"Your father...he collapsed," she lied, her voice shaking with false concern. "They're saying it might be a heart attack."

"Who is this?" Gregory demanded, his tone cold and suspicious.

"I work for the paramedics," Casey countered, her mind racing to stay one step ahead of him. "You need to get back to the city. Now."

"Nah. He's fine. He'll take care of himself. he always does."

She could tell he was on the verge of hanging up.

"Gregory, listen to me!" she cried out, desperation lending her voice an edge of raw emotion. "Your father needs you. Don't make a mistake you'll regret for the rest of your life."

The line went silent for what felt like an eternity, and Casey held her breath, praying that her ruse had worked. As she waited for his response, she pushed the car even faster, the rain-soaked roads stretching out before her like a gauntlet. Time was running out, and she knew it - but she refused to let the darkness claim Gabbie without a fight.

Rain battered the windshield relentlessly, as if trying to shatter Casey's resolve along with the glass.

The line crackled with tension, a tangible tightrope stretching between them.

"Where's my father now?" he asked, his indifference palpable even through the phone.

"Being taken care of," Casey replied, trying to keep her voice steady. She could hear the wariness in his words as he questioned her. "You should come to the hospital immediately."

"Right," Gregory drawled, the sarcasm evident in his response.

"Gregory," Casey implored, desperation leaking into her voice. Her pulse raced, her synesthetic senses painting the conversation in shades of crimson and indigo. "This isn't a joke. Your father needs you."

"Listen," he said sharply, annoyance dripping from every syllable. "I don't have time for games."

"Please—" Casey cut herself off, swallowing hard, forcing herself to sound like a concerned healthcare worker rather than an FBI agent on a mission. "I understand, but it's really urgent."

"Fine," Gregory sighed, his voice heavy with frustration. "Text me the details."

With that, he hung up, leaving Casey alone with only the relentless rain pelting against the windshield for company. Her heart sank as she realized that the distraction might not have been enough.

It seemed unlikely he would care at all if she texted him.

His voice had been one of indifference and irritation.

This, she hoped, was a good sign.

If he was irritated, and if he felt pressed for time, maybe his mother was still alive.

She urged the car forward, tracking the GPS dot on her phone--her turn was coming up.

She took the corner with a sharp twist, the tires screeching against the slick pavement. The country club loomed in front of her, a sprawling estate nestled among the trees. Casey's heart raced as she pulled up to the gate, the rain battering against the roof of the car.

She spotted a lone vehicle in the parking lot. Not the jeep.

But that didn't mean Gregory hadn't used the jeep in the past.

Clearly, the club wasn't meant to be open in the morning--or perhaps it was just the weather. She could see pickle ball courts, empty, slick and soaked.

She pushed from her car, approaching the closed, metal gate, peering towards the main building. Ivy twisted up the front of the faux stone facade.

Rain pummeled her, and within seconds she was soaked to the bone.

The cold touch of the water against her skin caused her heightened senses to slip into high gear. Her mind was a cloud of firing synapses.

Casey grabbed onto the gate, her fingers slipping from the wet metal. She tried again, and this time she was able to get a grip.

She hauled herself up, her sneakers slipping against the rain-slicked surface as she scrambled for purchase.

Her arms burned with exhaustion as she pulled herself higher and higher, her eyes focused on the top of the gate.

The rain continued to fall in sheets, coating every inch of Casey in water. Her clothes were sodden and clung heavily to her body, making it difficult for her to move.

Finally, after what felt like an eternity, Casey reached the top of the gate and swung one leg over. She paused for a moment before throwing her other leg over and dropping down into the parking lot below.

She stumbled forward over a puddle of mud and muck that had accumulated in the corner of the lot. She looked up at the sky above-- the storm clouds were still there, glaring down at her.

Shaking off some of the mud from her shoes, Casey trudged ahead towards the main building.

It was dark.

No sign of light or life.

She shivered, reached the front door, hesitated, and pushed.

Unlocked.

The door opened slowly into the dark.

CHAPTER TWENTY SIX

Her gloved hand rested on the rain-slicked handle to the country club, but she only kept it ajar for a second, listening intently.

No sounds from within.

Outside, the lightning streaked across the sky, illuminating the dark clouds that rolled above like ocean waves. Heavy rain cascaded from the heavens, drenching Casey to the bone. Her clothes clung to her body like a second skin, and she could feel rivulets of water streaming down her face. The wind howled around her.

She peered through the gap in the door, her gun now in her off-hand.

No sign of movement from within.

Was Gregory here?

Was his mother already dead?

The country club building loomed like a fortress amidst the storm, its brick walls standing tall and proud against the onslaught of nature. Its windows were dark, save for the occasional flash of lightning that painted the panes with ghostly light. The isolation of the club was palpable, as if it were intentionally hidden away from society's prying eyes.

She glanced once more to the parking lot, calculating; she didn't want to rush in. She couldn't warn him she was coming, or he might kill his victim and flee.

To the side of the building, the solitary car sat in the otherwise empty parking lot. Its presence seemed out of place, a lone island amid the vast sea of asphalt. The sleek black vehicle was parked crookedly, as if hastily abandoned by its driver.

No movement there, either.

No reaction to the door opening--the sound of the storm would've alerted anyone in the entrance.

But she was alone.

For now.

She pushed the door inward.

"Here goes nothing," she whispered as she stepped inside, her senses immediately assaulted by the musty scent of old wood and damp upholstery. A shiver ran down her spine, and not just from the cold rain that still clung to her clothes.

As she ventured further into the darkness, her synesthetic perceptions began to paint a picture of her surroundings, with colors and textures weaving together in a tapestry of sensory information. It was both overwhelming and comforting – a familiar cacophony that helped her navigate through the unknown.

The country club's interior unfolded before Casey like a grandiose stage designed to showcase wealth and opulence. A massive chandelier, shimmering with crystal and brass, dangled precariously overhead, casting fragmented light across the marble floor. Plush velvet chairs and sofas flanked an ornate fireplace, its fire long extinguished, leaving only the faint scent of burnt wood lingering in the air.

But what caught Casey's attention most were the hunting trophies adorning the walls, their glassy eyes seeming to follow her every move. She felt a shudder run down her spine as she took in the macabre menagerie – deer heads mounted on polished plaques, stuffed foxes frozen mid-pounce, and even a gigantic grizzly bear rearing on its hind legs, its claws extended as if ready to strike.

As Casey cautiously moved deeper into the room, her synesthetic abilities began to intermingle with the eerie atmosphere. The cold marble underfoot was a deep, chilling blue that seemed to seep into her skin, while the velvet upholstery of the furniture glowed with rich, pulsating hues of crimson and gold. The darkness around her seemed to hum with energy, like a low-frequency vibration that she couldn't quite pinpoint.

Her senses heightened further, the sounds in the room taking on distinct shapes and colors in her perception. The creaks of the floorboards beneath her were jagged spikes of yellow and orange, while the echoes of her own breath appeared as soft, ephemeral wisps of lavender.

It might have been easy to become lost in the swirling colors and sensations, but she had a job to do. Gregory Whitmore was somewhere in this labyrinth of luxury and death, and she refused to let him slip through her fingers.

She continued to navigate the country club, each step a careful balance between determination and stealth. The hunting trophies loomed large around her, their presence both haunting and strangely motivating. She thought of all the lives Gregory had taken.

Casey's breaths were measured and quiet, her eyes darting through the darkness as she moved with catlike grace. The ornate wallpaper was a blur of shapes and colors that blended together in a seamless tapestry, but her synesthesia allowed her to pick apart the distinct textures and hues – the velvety reds and golds that seemed to pulse with intensity as they mirrored her own determination.

A sudden movement caught her eye, and Casey froze in place, her senses on high alert. She scanned the room, trying to discern the source of the motion, but all she could see were the looming hunting trophies, their dead eyes watching her from every corner.

A flutter of cloth by the open window.

She relaxed a bit, took a step forward, glancing down an adjoining hall, and froze.

She stared in horror.

But a second later, her thoughts caught up with her instincts, and she released a pent-up breath.

A massive stuffed grizzly bear loomed over her like an avenging specter. Its glassy eyes bore into her soul, and for a split second, her synesthetic senses went haywire, flooding her vision with a maelstrom of color and texture that left her reeling.

"Get a grip," she chided herself, blinking away the disorienting sensation as quickly as it had come. She knew there was no time to be wasted on fear or hesitation; Gregory was still out there, and she had to find him before it was too late.

The disorienting explosion of colors from the grizzly bear's glassy gaze began to dissipate, allowing Casey to regain her focus. As she did so, a faint creaking sound drifted through the oppressive darkness, catching her attention. It seemed to be emanating from above, and her instincts told her that there was more to this noise than just the settling of an old building.

"Second floor," she whispered to herself, her senses sharpening with anticipation. The sound had been too deliberate, too out of place amidst the silence that enveloped the country club.

Casey's grip on her gun tightened, the steel cool against her gloved hand as she dashed towards the staircase. Every fiber of her being screamed for her to move quickly, yet silently – a deadly balance that she had honed throughout her career.

Her heart pounded in her chest, each beat fueling her determination to find Gregory.

As she ascended the stairs, the creaking grew louder, sending shivers down her spine that had nothing to do with the storm raging outside. But fear would have to wait; now was the time for action, and she couldn't let her heightened senses overwhelm her.

She reached the second floor and entered a long hall with bare walls.

Casey's breathing was sharp, slicing through the silence like a serrated knife. The shallow breaths cut into her lungs, each one laced with a frigid edge. She held the air for a moment before releasing it, trying to muffle the sound as much as possible. Her heightened state of alertness demanded that every sense be fine-tuned, her body and mind working together in perfect harmony.

The gun in her gloved hand felt like an extension of her arm, its weight reassuring in its familiarity.

She peered down the long hall, and paused.

She frowned, inhaling slowly and detecting the scent of... chlorine?

A pool.

There was a pool at the end of the hall.

She took quick steps now, moving rapidly down the hallway, her footsteps muffled by the carpet along the floor which eventually gave way to white, lacquered tile.

And there, centering the wall opposite her was a viewing window, reflecting shimmering blue from the chlorinated pool.

She reached the window, peered through...

And froze.

The sight that confronted her robbed her breath away.

CHAPTER TWENTY SEVEN

Casey stood in the hall on the second floor, drenched and staring towards the figure visible through the window.

The viewing window overlooked an Olympic sized swimming pool, and her eyes widened at the sight before her.

It was the hot tub in the corner that caught her attention. A large hot tub, almost a small pool in itself.

But the hot tub didn't glisten blue like the pool.

The once-pristine water now rippled with dark, inky shades of red and blue. The smell of chlorine mixed with something metallic lingered in the air, making her stomach churn. She could taste the tension that permeated the room, like the bitter aftertaste of almonds on her tongue.

It was the man who most drew her attention; she stared at him as he moved along the edge of the pool.

Her gaze fixated on Gregory Whitmore as he wheeled a massive vat of wine towards the edge of the hot tub. The muscles in his arms strained under the weight of the container, sweat dripping from his brow and mingling with the cuts that marred his face. The crimson liquid inside the vat sloshed dangerously close to the rim, threatening to spill over with every step he took.

"Is he...?" Casey trailed off, unable to complete the thought, her heart pounding in her chest.

She watched intently as Gregory maneuvered the heavy vat into position, wondering what twisted purpose he had in mind. Each labored breath he took seemed to echo through the cavernous space, punctuating the eerie silence that hung heavy in the air. It felt as if time itself had slowed down, the anticipation building within Casey as she struggled to make sense of the scene before her.

Gregory's movements were deliberate, each one calculated. As the crimson liquid cascaded from the vat into the hot tub, the sound of splashing wine intertwined with the vigorous bubbling of water, creating a dissonant symphony that played on Casey's senses.

The sight was hauntingly mesmerizing; Casey couldn't tear her eyes away.

Her attention shifted abruptly as the slumped figure on a nearby bench came into view. Bound and unconscious, the woman seemed so pitiful, so vulnerable. A wave of empathy washed over Casey.

It was Gregory's mother.

Whitmore's wife lay unconscious, her hands bound.

The realization sent shivers down her spine, making her skin crawl beneath her long sleeves. Shock and revulsion mingled within her, vying for dominance as she struggled to process the horrifying scene before her.

The fluorescent lighting above cast a sickly glow on Gregory's face as he scratched at his skin, his fingers leaving angry red trails in its wake. The sound of nails scraping against flesh filled Casey's ears, making her cringe involuntarily.

"Must... be... perfect," Gregory muttered to himself, seemingly unaware of Casey's presence. His voice was strained and desperate, the words barely escaping through gritted teeth.

The sounds came through the ajar door, propped open by a red shim at her side.

He hadn't noticed her yet.

Casey's synesthetic perception allowed her to sense the discomfort Gregory felt about his appearance, manifesting as jagged shards of ice-blue in her vision. The intensity reminded her of the broken mirror she had discovered in Gregory's home, a shattered reflection of the man's fractured self-image. It was evident that his obsession with perfection had consumed him, twisting his mind into something dark and dangerous.

As he tipped the wine, his voice rose in volume, and Gregory was screaming now, though unaware he had an audience.

The room shuddered with the reverberations of Gregory's ranting, his voice a symphony of malice and anguish. He continued to wheel a second vat towards the hot tub, each rotation of the wheels accompanied by a hollow groan that resonated in the stale air.

"Justice must be served!" Gregory shouted to the empty room, his words echoing around him like a pack of malicious spirits. "The wicked shall suffer for their sins!"

As he poured the wine into the bubbling water, its crimson hue swirled and merged with the steam, forming a miasma of intoxicating torment.

Gregory seethed, "Your day of reckoning has come."

He turned to face his mother once the vat of wine had emptied.

No more time.

Casey pushed through the ajar door, summoning inner resolve. Her gun clutched in her gloved hands.

"Gregory Whitmore!" she bellowed, her voice slicing through the air like a silver bullet.

Her boots splashed against the wet tiles as she stepped into the pool area, weapon raised, ready to confront the monster that lurked within the man before her. In that instant, the world seemed to freeze, as if time itself held its breath in anticipation of what was to come.

"Stop right there!" Casey commanded, her words infused with a resolve.

Gregory's body tensed, and his eyes widened in surprise. He turned to look at her, horror in his gaze.

"Put the vat down, Gregory," Casey demanded. "You don't want to do this."

His gaze flicked between Casey and the unconscious figure of his mother, uncertainty warring with the fury that still coursed through his veins. A fleeting memory of their shattered mirror at home flashed in Casey's mind – a reminder of the broken soul she faced.

For a moment, the room hung suspended in a delicate balance between life and death, hope and despair. It was a dance upon a razor's edge.

"Stay where you are," she commanded, her voice steady and resolute. Gregory's face bore the marks of his frantic scratching, crimson lines weaving through his skin like a macabre tapestry. The scentless air around them seemed to buzz with tension, as if charged with invisible electricity.

"Stranger," Gregory whispered, his voice barely audible over the bubbling hot tub. "You don't understand. She deserves this."

"Nobody deserves what you're planning, Gregory," Casey retorted, taking measured strides towards him while keeping her weapon trained on his chest.

She used his name specifically, enunciating the word, hoping it might calm him. Her palms were slick with sweat beneath her gloves, but she refused to let fear seep into her words – the situation was dangerous enough without it.

"Please," he pleaded, his voice cracking with desperation. "I can't bear to see her like this anymore."

This didn't make sense.

At least, not at first.

But the scratches on his face told the story of his self-hatred. Was he punishing himself or his parents?

As Casey assessed the scene before her, she could feel the weight of decades' worth of pain radiating from Gregory. It was a suffocating sensation, one she shared with him due to her synesthetic perception. But she couldn't let empathy cloud her judgment; there was still a life at stake besides his own.

"We can find help for you, for your mother. You don't have to go down this path."

An odd smile twisted Gregory's lips, a grim mockery of amusement. "It's too late for that. I've already made my choice."

"Then choose again," she urged him, her heart aching for the broken man in front of her. "It's not too late to change your mind."

But Gregory remained unmoved, his eyes locked on Casey as if challenging her to deny the truth that coiled around them like a venomous serpent. And as the seconds ticked by, it became increasingly clear that the outcome of this deadly dance would be determined not by reason or compassion, but by the unyielding grip of fate itself.

Casey's heart pounded like a drumbeat, and she could feel her adrenaline surging through her veins. In this moment, it seemed as if the world had slowed to a crawl, with every detail standing out in stark relief. The way Gregory's nails dug into his palms, the tiny beads of sweat dotting his forehead, and the bitter tang of fear that clung to the air.

His eyes flickered for an instant, a storm of emotions swirling within their depths – anger, despair, and something else she couldn't quite name. And then, without warning, he lunged.

"NO!" Casey screamed, her panic mingling with the raw terror that filled the room as Gregory closed the distance between himself and his mother. The knife glinted in his hand like a deadly beacon, its blade a promise of violence that sent shivers down Casey's spine.

In that split second, her instincts kicked into overdrive. She raised her gun, her finger tightening on the trigger with practiced precision. The gunshot echoed through the room, and she saw Gregory's shoulder jerk back from the impact as crimson bloomed against his shirt.

But it wasn't enough to stop him. His small frame, fueled by desperation and madness, continued its menacing advance, closing in on the helpless woman bound to the bench.

No time for doubt, no time for hesitation. Casey's mind raced, searching for a way to end this nightmare without further bloodshed. Her senses, heightened by her synesthesia, were both a blessing and a curse, allowing her to perceive the situation in ways others couldn't, but also threatening to overwhelm her with the cacophony of colors, sounds, and sensations.

The knife's razor edge, glinting in the dim light, pressed against his mother's pale, vulnerable neck. Gregory's eyes, wild and frenzied, locked onto Casey's steady gaze. She could see the battle raging within him, a struggle of wills and survival, as his grip on the hilt tightened.

"Please," his mother whispered, her voice trembling with fear, barely audible above the sound of blood pounding in Casey's ears.

She was only semi-conscious, blinking and trying to rouse herself.

"Quiet!" Gregory snarled, the veins in his neck standing out like cords.

Casey's gloved fingers tightened around her gun, but she knew any sudden moves would spell disaster. The colors of the room swirled around her, an abstract painting of tension and chaos born from her synesthesia. Her senses were both amplified and muddled, making it difficult for her to maintain focus. She had to maintain control lest the sensory onslaught cloud her judgment and compromise her ability to save this woman.

She needed to calm him, to get him to speak to her, to remove his focus from his mother, from the source of his hatred.

Whenever he looked at her face, he grew angrier, so she drew his attention to her.

Casey wasn't even sure what she was saying; she mostly just reached for words, desperate to distract.

"Gregory, I understand you're angry, but hurting your mother won't change anything," Casey reasoned, her voice calm yet firm. "Put the knife down, and we can talk."

"Talk?" He spat the word out like venom, his blue eyes blazing with fury. "There's nothing left to say."

As they faced each other, the air between them seemed to thicken, heavy with the weight of desperation and the potential for violence.

"Think about what you're doing," she urged, trying to reach the humanity buried beneath his rage, while still drawing his attention. She stepped slightly to the side, gun raised, trying to find a clear angle. "If you hurt your mother, there's no coming back from that. You don't want that on your conscience for the rest of your life."

"Shut up!" Gregory's voice cracked, revealing a vulnerability that Casey grasped onto like a lifeline. "You don't know anything about me or my life!"

"Maybe not," she admitted, her grip on the gun steady despite the tremors that threatened to overtake her. "But think. Just *think*!

The world around them seemed to hold its breath, suspended in time, as their eyes remained locked in an intense battle of wills. Every fiber of Casey's being strained with anticipation, waiting for Gregory's next move, praying it would be one of surrender rather than violence.

"Please," his mother whispered again, her eyes brimming with tears.

Gregory's eyes flicked to his mother, then back to Casey, and she could see the tremor in his hand as he held the knife.

CHAPTER TWENTY EIGHT

"Gregory, please, let's talk about this," Casey pleaded, her voice soft and steady, despite the pounding of her heart in her chest. She could feel the rapid thump-thump of her pulse in her fingertips, even through the thin fabric of her gloves.

"Shut up!" Gregory snapped, his eyes wild with rage and desperation as he pressed the knife closer to his mother's throat. Crimson droplets welled up around the blade, threatening to spill over onto the woman's pale skin. The bubbling hot tub of wine nearby cast an eerie red glow on their faces, heightening the surreal horror of the scene unfolding before Casey.

"You don't want to do this," Casey insisted, trying to keep her voice calm as she tightened her grip on the gun, aiming it squarely at him. Her dark hair remained pulled back in a tight ponytail, keeping her senses clear and unobstructed.

"Like hell I don't," Gregory spat. "She deserves everything that's coming to her. Do you know who they are? What they've done! I had to be perfect! Goddamn perfect!" He screamed. One hand reached up, scratching at his already marred face.

Casey's mind raced as she searched for the right words, anything that might reach through Gregory's anger and make him see reason. "Think about what you're doing here, Gregory. Hurting your mother won't solve anything. We can get you help, but you need to put the knife down."

"Help?" Gregory sneered, his eyes narrowing into dangerous slits. "There's no helping me, not after what she's done!"

"Don't destroy both your lives over something that can be fixed."

"Fixed?" Gregory's laugh was bitter and hollow. "There's no fixing this. This is who I am because of her!"

The scent of chlorine wafted through the air, a harsh chemical contrast to the rich, earthy aroma of the bubbling wine. It swirled around Casey, mingling with the thick tension and fear that hung heavy in the atmosphere. She could feel it pressing down on her, a smothering blanket threatening to suffocate her thoughts.

She glanced at the bubbling hot tub, its surface shimmering like liquid rubies beneath the flickering light. The scent of chlorine grew stronger as she focused on the pool, using it to ground herself, to anchor her thoughts amid the swirling chaos.

Gregory stood before her, his face twisted into a snarl, his fingers white-knuckled around the knife pressed against his mother's throat.

"Drop the gun," he hissed, his voice cracking with desperation. "Or I swear to God I'll slit her throat right here, right now."

Casey's eyes flicked between the blade and the fear-filled gaze of the bound woman.

As his tirade continued, Casey took advantage of his distraction, shifting her weight onto the balls of her feet. Another inch to the right.

Another.

She needed a clear shot.

His eyes widened, though. As if he realized what she intended.

His hand on the knife tightened.

Her heart sank.

She'd tried to warn him. Tried to keep him from crossing a line from which there was no return.

But it was of no use.

She didn't like hurting anyone. Not even killers.

But he was leaving her no choice. Either she hurt him through action, or hurt his mother through inaction.

And so, as he tightened his grip on the knife, she took a final step to the right, clearing her line of fire, one foot on the very edge of the hot tub.

She pulled the trigger.

The gunshot echoed through the pool like thunder, its reverberations shaking the very air itself. Casey's ears rang with the deafening roar, but she forced herself to remain focused, her eyes locked on Gregory.

For a moment, it seemed as though time had stopped, the world holding its breath in anticipation. And then, just as suddenly, time lurched forward again, reality snapping back into place.

Gregory's eyes widened with shock, his grip on the knife faltering as pain and disbelief washed over him. The weapon clattered to the ground, its fall punctuated by a metallic clang that rang out like a death knell.

"Wh-What did you...?" he gasped, his voice barely a whisper as he stumbled back, red now streaming down his arm. His shoulder was also bleeding from the earlier wound.

In the stillness that followed the gunshot, Casey's senses sharpened. The taste of gunpowder hung heavy in the air, sharp and bitter on her tongue. Colors swirled around her, the deep red hues of the wine in the hot tub seeming to dance like flames as they mingled with the scent of chlorine from the nearby pool.

For a second, she thought he'd fall back.

But his lips twisted into a snarl. He glared at her, breathing heavily. And he reached for his knife, which had clattered to the ground.

She had a second to make a choice.

Another bullet, straight to the chest, and he'd be down.

But...

She cursed, and launched herself forward, forgoing the open shot.

It was a risky move; Nathan would've berated her if he'd seen it.

But there'd already been so much death.

Mercy... it was a horrible notion to many who didn't own a mirror.

She had to stop him. But in that brief instance, she thought she could do it without another bullet.

With a burst of movement, she tackled Gregory, her body crashing into his like a tidal wave before he could reach his knife.

He grunted, his eyes widening in surprise as he struggled beneath her, desperately trying to regain control.

"Get off me!" he snarled, his face contorting with rage and humiliation. "You have no right—"

"Enough," Casey growled, her grip tightening around his wrists. She felt a surge of determination fueled by the memories of those who had suffered at his hands.

At their side, where they struggle on the ground, the hot tub's surface rippled, the burgundy waves reflecting the eerie glow of the vineyard's dim lights. Casey's breath hitched in her throat as she held onto Gregory, his body thrashing with wild desperation beneath her grip.

"Let me go!" he screamed, his voice a guttural snarl of fury and anguish. "You have no idea what it's like!"

His muscles tensed beneath her grasp, and with a sudden burst of strength, he wrenched himself free from her grip.

But she lashed out again, roping an arm around his stomach.

The two of them tumbled forward together. Their bodies collided, crashing into the hot tub full of wine with a splash that sent droplets soaring through the air.

CHAPTER TWENTY NINE

Casey struggle to orient herself in the hot tub full of wine and steam. It felt surreal, and her senses were overloaded.

The sound of splashing, cursing, the rivulets of red seeping around her all threatened to short-circuit her already frayed sensory experience.

With the addition of the wine, the hot tub was deeper than she'd first thought, and she was only barely standing.

The length of the hot tub was almost as long as a small pool to begin with.

And now, as steam clouded her vision, she spotted a silhouette charging towards her, a screech on his lips.

Gregory came at her, and somehow, he'd recovered his knife.

The heat was overwhelming. The water having soaked through her already rain-sodden clothing. Her hair plastered to her head, but she tracked the oncoming Gregory, and waiting until the last moment, she lashed out, catching his arm.

He cursed, spitting in her face.

He was a thin man, but still strong. And as she twisted his wrist, the knife fell free.

He howled in her face, spittle joining flecks of water. His arm was bleeding, and his right arm was a limp thing at his side.

She fought desperately to avoid being shoved into the water.

The knife hit the liquid at her side from where she'd twisted his wrist, disappearing.

But now his hands were scrambling towards her throat.

He was screaming at her, spitting and yelling and striking with desperation.

His fingers wrapped around her throat. They thrashed in the water. It sloshed over the edges, spreading out like a wave of crimson on the tiled floor.

And then, his foot hooked hers, and the two of them crashed into the depths under the veil of water.

For a moment, her senses were muted.

Water in her eyes, ears, nostrils.

She couldn't see, breathe. His fingers were still wrapped around her neck as he bore down on her, trying to drown her.

She kicked and clawed.

The two of them were caught in a dance under the water.

But she resisted, her hands flailing and pushing him away.

The two of them fought in the depths, their bodies twisting and turning in an intricate dance of survival.

She could feel his oxygen bubbles on her face as he tried to push her down, but she fought back with a ferocity borne from desperation.

He was strong, and so was she. But the water was an equalizer, making it so that neither one had an advantage over the other.

All while the wine moved around them like a river of red.

Finally, Casey managed to break free of Gregory's grip. She kicked off from him with all her strength, propelling herself up towards the surface before taking a deep breath when she broke through the waterline.

Gregory stayed below, his body still and unmoving beneath the surface as Casey gasped for air and surveyed her surroundings.

He snatched at her leg all of a sudden, trying to pull her down. Though the water was warm, it wasn't scalding, but he was still struggling to see as well in the murk.

Whereas Casey was no longer using her eyesight for her primary sense.

She *felt* the ripple of the current against her skin and *felt* the way he moved. Where he was.

She didn't need to see that he was scrambling with one hand for the knife on the tiled floor.

She stomped out, and he loosed a silent scream which released bubbles under the water.

She grabbed at his ear, twisting.

She yanked to the side of the tub.

And now, her ability to track his movements even without the use of her sight--her eyes clouded in mist, chlorine and thrashing water-- gave her the advantage she needed.

She herded him back, back, back against the edge of the tub.

He was weakening now.

And new streams of red in the water hinted that blood loss was a part of it just as much as anything else.

She gave him a final shove, and he slumped against the edge of the pool, gasping.

The fight seemed to have left him. His face was pale.

Casey grabbed a hold of him, her grip tight as she dragged him out of the water.

She scrambled onto the edge of the hot tub, breathing heavily, soaked to the bone.

He just moaned, wheezing on the ground.

She cuffed his hands behind his back, and he lay there on the tiles, exhausted.

Casey leaned against the side of the pool, her breathing heavy as she surveyed the scene.

The air was still and silent, apart from their labored breaths.

The red liquid had spread everywhere, creating a macabre mosaic on the tiles that seemed to stretch beyond what could be seen with just her eyes. The smell of chlorine mixed with blood filled her nostrils and made her gag.

But Casey closed her eyes and took a deep breath. She had done it. She had managed to stop Gregory from taking away another life.

Including his own.

Wearily, she pushed to her feet, and, stumbling--exhausted--she approached the bound woman.

"Mrs. Whitmore, it's going to be okay," she said, gently.

Tears streamed down the woman's face, and in the distance, the sound of approaching sirens whispered of the civilization that lurked just beyond these halls of horror.

CHAPTER THIRTY

The precinct buzzed with life, officers and detectives scurrying about like worker bees in a hive. Casey Bolt stood beside Nathan Hayes, their shoulders touching, the air between them electrified with relief. The case that had consumed their every waking moment was finally closed.

Casey rubbed her eyes, turning specifically away from the booking sergeant who was waiting for the paramedics to call the station.

Gregory would survive.

The same couldn't be said for his parents' emotional health.

Casey shook her head, closing her eyes and releasing a long, pent-up breath.

She threw the pen she'd used to sign the processing papers back into the cup holder and began moving towards the door once more.

At her side, Nathan--who'd been the first to show up at the scene after Gregory had been cuffed--exhaled deeply, his shoulders relaxing as the weight of the case lifted from them. He glanced over at Casey, his dark eyes softening with concern. The lines on his rugged face, a testament to his years as an undercover cop, seemed to dissipate momentarily as he focused on her well-being.

"Are you alright?" he asked, his voice gentle.

Casey nodded, but Nathan's gaze lingered, searching for any sign of distress. She forced a tired smile, knowing he wouldn't stop worrying until he was certain she was okay. As if sensing her need for comfort, he reached out and gave her gloved hand a reassuring squeeze.

"Seriously, I'm fine," she insisted, her voice barely above a whisper. "We did it, Nathan. We got him."

He returned her smile, but it was tinged with sadness. He knew the cost of this victory, the sacrifices they'd both made along the way.

"Yeah, we did," he said, nodding. "But it doesn't make it any less difficult."

The room around them continued to hum with activity, but for a brief moment, time seemed to stand still as Casey allowed herself to drink in the sight of Nathan's relieved expression. Her synesthesia flared, painting the edges of her vision with hues of purple and green.

A kaleidoscope of colors swirled before Casey's eyes as she took in the bustling precinct around her. The intensity of the case had brought her synesthesia to new heights, making it difficult for her to discern between reality and the vivid hues her mind painted. She felt a mixture of relief, exhaustion, and something else she couldn't quite place...

"Hey, you sure you're okay?" Nathan asked again, his voice pulling her from her thoughts. He scratched the back of his head.

"Y-yeah," Casey stammered, swallowing hard as she met his gaze. "I'm just... processing everything."

"Me too," he replied with a small nod. "You shouldn't have gone off like that."

"I know."

"I mean it."

She smiled. "I know."

"Listen," Nathan started, his voice soft and hesitant. "I know we've been through a lot with this case, but I want you to know that I've got your back, Casey. No matter what."

Casey felt her heart swell at his words, the sincerity in his eyes sending a shiver down her spine. She didn't know how to respond, but she found herself nodding in gratitude, her throat constricting with emotion.

"Thanks, Nathan," she managed to whisper, her voice cracking ever so slightly. "That means a lot to me."

She wasn't even sure where the emotion had suddenly come from.

Perhaps it was simply exhaustion, but it didn't stop her from stepping forward and giving her partner a quick hug.

He tensed briefly, but then returned the gesture.

"Let's get out of here, huh?" Nathan suggested, his voice sounding a bit shaky. "We both could use some rest."

"Sounds good," Casey agreed, her breath hitching as she met his gaze.

They walked out of the precinct together.

***

Night came quickly, and anticipation built as she stared at her phone.

Sure. When?

Had she really sent it.

152

Yes... There it was. Indelibly etched into the pixels.

She'd responded to Zach's dating request.

She sighed, closing her eyes.

What had suddenly made her long for the attention of a partner... A romantic partner. Nothing like... nothing like any *other* type.

She frowned, shaking her head.

Time seemed to ebb and flow in a strange, languid pattern as Casey waited for Zach's response. Night had fallen like a heavy curtain over the city, the once bustling streets now draped in shadows and silence. Streetlights cast amber pools of light onto the wet pavement, their reflections shimmering against the dark canvas. A cool breeze whispered through the air, carrying with it the crisp scent of autumn leaves.

Casey found herself standing by her apartment window, her gloved hands pressed against the cold glass. The night sky was a deep indigo, dotted with distant stars that she could barely make out through the haze of the city. Her thoughts, however, remained firmly anchored in the present, refusing to drift away into the endless expanse above.

"Come on," she muttered under her breath, her eyes flicking nervously to her phone lying on the coffee table. "Just respond, one way or the other."

Her synesthesia painted the tension in her chest in shades of violet and blue, a nebulous cloud of emotions clashing with the vivid colors of anticipation and anxiety. She tried to focus on the calming hues of the night sky, but they were constantly overshadowed by the turmoil within.

The sudden chime of her phone startled her, sending electric jolts of adrenaline coursing through her veins. She rushed to pick it up.

"Hello?" she said, her voice tight with apprehension.

"Casey?"

She went still.

"D-dad?"

This was an unexpected call.

Her grip on the phone tightened involuntarily, the smooth plastic suddenly feeling like jagged ice against her skin. Her father – a ghost from her past that she hadn't heard from in any meaningful capacity in years – now reaching out across the void with an urgency that sent shivers down her spine.

"Wh-what do you want?" she stammered, her mind racing to process the implications of his sudden reappearance.

"Casey, I need your help," he said, his voice strained and filled with an emotion she couldn't quite place. "It's about your mother's case. Something's come up, and...and I don't know who else to turn to."

She stood there, frozen in disbelief. The words hung in the air like a question mark, their jagged edges embedding themselves into the fabric of her consciousness. Casey's thoughts raced through the myriad possibilities that could have prompted her father's call, each more chilling than the last.

"News?" Casey echoed, her surprise morphing into curiosity. She could feel the colors of her synesthesia swirling around her like an amalgam of confusion and apprehension. "What do you mean?"

"Something happened," her father replied hesitantly, as if unsure how much to reveal. "I saw an article that mentioned your mother's case. It's been years since we've heard anything about it. I thought...maybe you'd want to know."

Casey's chest tightened at the mention of her mother's case - a wound that had never quite healed, despite the passage of time. Her mind raced, trying to piece together the puzzle her father was laying out before her.

"Okay," she said, taking a deep breath and attempting to steady herself. "Tell me what you know."

Her father hesitated for a moment, the silence on the other end of the line ringing with uncertainty. "I think it would be better if we met in person," he suggested, his voice barely audible. "There's too much to explain over the phone. Can you meet me tomorrow morning? At that old diner we used to go to?"

The colors surrounding Casey grew darker, more intense, as suspicion crept into her thoughts. Why did he need to see her in person? What secrets lay hidden within her mother's case that had suddenly resurfaced after all these years?

"Alright," she conceded, her voice wavering slightly with trepidation. "Tomorrow morning. But, Dad, if this is some kind of trick or something--"

"I promise, Casey," he interrupted, his tone firm yet pleading. "This is important. I wouldn't have called if it wasn't."

"Fine," she agreed, though her gut churned with unease. "I'll see you there."

"Thank you, Casey," her father breathed out, the relief in his voice palpable. "I love you."

"Goodbye, Dad," she replied softly, unable to return the sentiment just yet. As she ended the call, a heavy silence settled over her small apartment.

Casey stared at her phone, the screen now dark and unassuming. Yet, it held the key to a mystery that had haunted her for years – one that she would have to face head-on if she ever hoped to find peace.

As she turned off the lights and crawled into bed, her thoughts swirled with questions and uncertainties, like an ominous storm brewing on the horizon.

NOW AVAILABLE!

FLAWED
(A Casey Bolt FBI Suspense Thriller—Book Two)

FBI special agent Casey Bolt, with her rare neurological condition, is able to see and feel patterns other can't. When a renowned textile artist is found murdered on the remote San Juan islands, the only clue is a cryptic message woven into fabric, and Casey must tap her special skill to follow the trail and hunt down a diabolical killer— before he strikes again.

"Molly Black has written a taut thriller that will keep you on the edge of your seat... I absolutely loved this book and can't wait to read the next book in the series!"
—Reader review for Girl One: Murder

FLAWED is book #2 of a long anticipated new series by critically-acclaimed and #1 bestselling mystery and suspense author Molly Black, whose books have received over 2,000 five-star reviews and ratings.

Casey, grappling with synesthesia, has the rare ability to perceive senses in multiple ways, enabling her to view crime scenes, and track down clues, in ways others cannot. Her talent has made her indispensable to the FBI, but while her renown in the FBI grows, Casey remains tormented by the case that haunts her the most: her mother's brutal, unsolved murder from fifteen years ago.

As Casey strives to uncover the secrets of the past, she must rely on every instinct and insight to make it out of the field alive. But can her own senses lead her astray?

A page-turning and harrowing crime thriller featuring a brilliant and tortured FBI agent, the CASEY BOLT series is a riveting mystery, packed with non-stop action, suspense, twists and turns, revelations, and driven by a breakneck pace that will keep you flipping pages late into the night. Fans of Rachel Caine, Teresa Driscoll and Robert Dugoni are sure to fall in love.

Future books in the series are also available.

"I binge read this book. It hooked me in and didn't stop till the last few pages... I look forward to reading more!"
—Reader review for Found You

"I loved this book! Fast-paced plot, great characters and interesting insights into investigating cold cases. I can't wait to read the next book!"
—Reader review for Girl One: Murder

"Very good book... You will feel like you are right there looking for the kidnapper! I know I will be reading more in this series!"
—Reader review for Girl One: Murder

"This is a very well written book and holds your interest from page 1... Definitely looking forward to reading the next one in the series, and hopefully others as well!"
—Reader review for Girl One: Murder

"Wow, I cannot wait for the next in this series. Starts with a bang and just keeps going."
—Reader review for Girl One: Murder

"Well written book with a great plot, one that will keep you up at night. A page turner!"
—Reader review for Girl One: Murder

"A great suspense that keeps you reading... can't wait for the next in this series!"
—Reader review for Found You

"Sooo soo good! There are a few unforeseen twists... I binge read this like I binge watch Netflix. It just sucks you in."
—Reader review for Found You

Molly Black

Bestselling author Molly Black is author of the MAYA GRAY FBI suspense thriller series, comprising ten books (and counting); of the RYLIE WOLF FBI suspense thriller series, comprising six books; of the TAYLOR SAGE FBI suspense thriller series, comprising eight books; of the KATIE WINTER FBI suspense thriller series, comprising eleven books (and counting); of the RUBY HUNTER FBI suspense thriller series, comprising five books (and counting); of the CAITLIN DARE FBI suspense thriller series, comprising six books (and counting); of the REESE LINK mystery series, comprising six books (and counting); of the CLAIRE KING FBI suspense thriller series, comprising seven books (and counting); of the PIPER WOODS mystery series, comprising five books (and counting); of the GRACE FORD mystery series, comprising seven books (and counting); and of the CASEY BOLT mystery series, comprising five books (and counting).

An avid reader and lifelong fan of the mystery and thriller genres, Molly loves to hear from you, so please feel free to visit www.mollyblackauthor.com to learn more and stay in touch.

BOOKS BY MOLLY BLACK

CASEY BOLT MYSTERY SERIES
BROKEN (Book #1)
FLAWED (Book #2)
BLEMISHED (Book #3)
DAMAGED (Book #4)
TWISTED (Book #5)

GRACE FORD MYSTERY SERIES
NEARLY MINE (Book #1)
NEARLY SAFE (Book #2)
NEARLY FREE (Book #3)
NEARLY GONE (Book #4)
NEARLY HIS (Book #5)

CLAIRE KING MYSTERY SERIES
ONCE HE SEES (Book #1)
ONCE HE LONGS (Book #2)
ONCE HE TAKES (Book #3)
ONCE HE FEELS (Book #4)
ONCE HE KNOWS (Book #5)

MAYA GRAY MYSTERY SERIES
GIRL ONE: MURDER (Book #1)
GIRL TWO: TAKEN (Book #2)
GIRL THREE: TRAPPED (Book #3)
GIRL FOUR: LURED (Book #4)
GIRL FIVE: BOUND (Book #5)
GIRL SIX: FORSAKEN (Book #6)
GIRL SEVEN: CRAVED (Book #7)
GIRL EIGHT: HUNTED (Book #8)
GIRL NINE: GONE (Book #9)

RYLIE WOLF FBI SUSPENSE THRILLER
FOUND YOU (Book #1)
CAUGHT YOU (Book #2)

SEE YOU (Book #3)
WANT YOU (Book #4)
TAKE YOU (Book #5)
DARE YOU (Book #6)

TAYLOR SAGE FBI SUSPENSE THRILLER
DON'T LOOK (Book #1)
DON'T BREATHE (Book #2)
DON'T RUN (Book #3)
DON'T FLINCH (Book #4)
DON'T REMEMBER (Book #5)
DON'T TELL (Book #6)

KATIE WINTER FBI SUSPENSE THRILLER
SAVE ME (Book #1)
REACH ME (Book #2)
HIDE ME (Book #3)
BELIEVE ME (Book #4)
HELP ME (Book #5)
FORGET ME (Book #6)
HOLD ME (Book #7)
PROTECT ME (Book #8)
REMEMBER ME (Book #9)
CATCH ME (Book #10)
WATCH ME (Book #11)

RUBY HUNTER FBI SUSPENSE THRILLER
IF I RUN (Book #1)
IF I TELL (Book #2)
IF I LIVE (Book #3)
IF I FORGET (Book #4)
IF I RETURN (Book #5)

CAITLIN DARE FBI SUSPENSE THRILLER
COME GET ME (Book #1)
COME FIND ME (Book #2)
COME TAKE ME (Book #3)
COME CATCH ME (Book #4)
COME SAVE ME (Book #5)

REESE LINK MYSTERY

Made in the USA
Coppell, TX
26 December 2023

26854093R00095